"Did I pass the An edge of anger definitely laced his words.

"I never meant your talk with Jakie to be a test. I just want what's best for my son," Faith replied.

"But it was."

"You handled Jakie very well."

Laying his hands on her shoulders, Nick said, "I would never do anything to hurt that boy."

"I know you wouldn't." After seeing him with Jakie today, hearing them talk, she was sure of it.

Nick must have heard the certainty. The tense lines around his eyes lessened, and the look in them gentled. He kept studying her face as if he was searching for something. She wanted him to kiss her again. Why couldn't she be forward? Why couldn't she just reach out...?

Dear Reader,

The holiday season is a time for family, love...and miracles! We have all this—and more!—for you this month in Silhouette Romance. So in the gift-giving spirit, we offer *you* these wonderful books by some of the genre's finest:

A workaholic executive finds a baby in his in-box and enlists the help of the sexy single mom next door in this month's BUNDLES OF JOY, *The Baby Came C.O.D.*, by RITA Award-winner Marie Ferrarella. *Both* hero and heroine are twins, and Marie tells their identical siblings' stories in *Desperately Seeking Twin*, out this month in our Yours Truly line.

Favorite author Elizabeth August continues our MEN! promotion with *Paternal Instincts*. This latest installment in her SMYTHESHIRE, MASSACHUSETTS series features an irresistible lone wolf turned doting dad! As a special treat, Carolyn Zane's sizzling family drama, THE BRUBAKER BRIDES, continues with *His Brother's Intended Bride*—the title says it all!

Completing the month are *three* classic holiday romances. A world-weary hunk becomes *The Dad Who Saved Christmas* in this magical tale by Karen Rose Smith. Discover *The Drifter's Gift* in RITA Award-winning author Lauryn Chandler's emotional story. Finally, debut author Zena Valentine weaves a tale of transformation—and miracles—in *From Humbug to Holiday Bride*.

So treat yourself this month—and every month!—to Silhouette Romance!

Happy holidays,

Joan Marlow Golan
Senior Editor

Please address questions and book requests to:
Silhouette Reader Service
U.S.: 3010 Walden Ave., P.O. Box 1325, Buffalo, NY 14269
Canadian: P.O. Box 609, Fort Erie, Ont. L2A 5X3

THE DAD WHO SAVED CHRISTMAS

Karen Rose Smith

Nancy,
May your Christmas
be filled with warm
memories and good friends.

All my best,
Karen Rose Smith

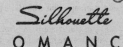

Silhouette

ROMANCE™

Published by Silhouette Books

America's Publisher of Contemporary Romance

In loving memory of my father, Angelo Jacob Cacciola,
1916-1989.
I love you and miss you, Daddy.
Author's Note: Adoption procedures may vary according
to individual circumstances and agencies.

 SILHOUETTE BOOKS

ISBN 0-373-19267-3

THE DAD WHO SAVED CHRISTMAS

Copyright © 1997 by Karen Rose Smith

Books by Karen Rose Smith

Silhouette Romance

Adam's Vow #1075
Always Daddy #1102
Shane's Bride #1128
†*Cowboy at the Wedding* #1171
†*Most Eligible Dad* #1174
†*A Groom and a Promise* #1181
The Dad Who Saved Christmas #1267

*Darling Daddies
†The Best Men

Silhouette Special Edition

Abigail and Mistletoe #930
The Sheriff's Proposal #1074

Previously published under the pseudonym Kari Sutherland

Silhouette Romance

Heartfire, Homefire #973

Silhouette Special Edition

Wish on the Moon #741

KAREN ROSE SMITH

enjoys writing books that are set during the holidays.
The magic of the season always spills into her characters
and settings. She believes the best part of Christmas is
spending time with family, renewing friendships.
Readers can write to her at P.O. Box 1545, Hanover, PA
17331. She wishes everyone a wonderful holiday season
filled with peace and special moments.

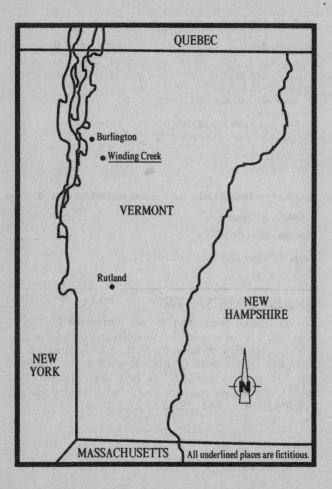

QUEBEC

● Burlington
● <u>Winding Creek</u>

VERMONT

Rutland
●

NEW
HAMPSHIRE

NEW
YORK

N

MASSACHUSETTS   All underlined places are fictitious.

Chapter One

Snow blindness.

The flakes hit Nicholas Clark's windshield with a ferocity he didn't expect. Living in Vermont, he was used to snow. And on his way to a ski resort three hours from Rutland, he even looked forward to it. But for the past hour he'd driven in near blizzard conditions. As his sedan swerved in the six inches of white powder, he knew he'd have to stop soon if he didn't want to get stranded by the side of the road.

The only problem was he'd passed the sign telling him he was entering the town of Winding Creek. Winding Creek was the last place in the world he wanted to get waylaid. He'd lived in the small town his first nineteen years and had left without looking back.

But fate always had a way of interfering with the best laid plans.

His stomach growled and, in the last dim light of day, he realized he needed food and shelter whether he wanted to be in Winding Creek or not.

He recognized a restaurant that had been the haunt of teenagers when he was in high school. Everything in Winding Creek defied change. That's why he'd left.

Flakes of snow fell on his hair and his sweater as he climbed out of his car and trekked to the restaurant's entrance. But before he could go in, an elderly man burst from the building next door. "Hey. We need help. We got a young 'un hanging in the air and no one tall enough to reach him."

Nick heard the panic in the man's voice and hurried after him into an older building that used to be a warehouse. As he went inside, he read the plaque on the door—Winding Creek Community Center.

The large room with its tan linoleum, cafeteria-style tables and stage at the far end, was bedlam. A few women, but mostly children, were talking and pointing to a little boy dangling from a harness in midair, about ten feet off the ground, in the center of the two-foot-high stage.

Grabbing a chair, Nick didn't bother with the steps alongside the stage, but vaulted directly onto it mid-center, chair and all. The child swinging in the harness didn't look scared, just a bit perplexed by all the excitement. Nick gauged the boy's age to be around five. Since Nick owned a toy store, he was familiar with children of all ages and sizes.

It was ironic he'd been headed for the ski lodge to escape squabbling kids, irritable parents and the trappings of a commercial Christmas and landed in the middle of...

"Don't yank on the rope."

"Tell him to keep still."

"I'll try to find a ladder in the basement."

Amid the chaos and shouted instructions, a soft voice

soothed, "Don't be frightened, Jakie. I'm right here and I won't let anything happen to you."

In its quiet truth, the woman's voice sounded above all the others. At least for Nick. And for the little boy who Nick supposed was pretending to be an angel. When his gaze fell on the young woman with light brown hair and the darkest brown eyes he'd ever seen, he realized he knew her. At least he had in high school. He'd never dated her, though he'd wanted to. But a boy from the wrong side of the tracks didn't date a girl like Faith.

She recognized him immediately. "Nick Clark?"

"None other," he said with a wry smile as he tore his gaze from hers and set up the chair under the child. "Hold on, sport. I'll have you down in a minute."

The little boy informed him, "The rope's stuck. They can't get me down."

Nick clasped Jakie under his arms and lifted him from the harness. A moment later, he'd set the boy on the stage.

Faith took the child in her arms and gave him a huge hug. "Are you all right?"

"Sure. Angels are supposed to fly," he said with a grin that made the freckles on his nose seem to dance. With his reddish-brown hair and blue eyes, he was the littlest angel personified.

Faith looked up at Nick. "Thank you. I was trying to stay calm…"

"And doing a good job of it," Nick added, really looking at Faith Hewitt for the first time in many years. She'd matured into a woman with quiet beauty. Her slightly wavy hair framed her face the way he remembered it had so many years ago.

When she smiled at him, he felt the strangest sensation in his chest and a stab of desire that jolted him. With her arm still around Jakie, she said, "You probably don't remember me, but we went to school together. Faith Hewitt."

Nick glanced at Jakie. "You aren't married?"

Faith's cheeks grew rosy. "No, I'm not."

Faith Hewitt had been one of the girls in high school that he'd respected. She'd kept herself away from the party scene that had been so much a part of those years he'd played varsity football.

Obviously he'd embarrassed her. "I had no right to assume..."

Rising to her feet, she explained, "I'm Jakie's foster parent."

The elderly man who'd pulled Nick into the community center patted the boy's head. "I think we'll stand you on some steps in the back and forget about the harness."

"But I wanna fly!" Jakie protested.

Faith put her hand on his shoulder. "We'll make you the best wings you've ever seen and everyone will believe you can fly. That's what's important."

"Can I help make them?" he asked.

"Sure, you can. Now why don't you go get your coat and boots and we'll head home."

"I hope you don't live far," Nick remarked. "It isn't fit to drive or walk."

"I have my four-wheel drive. We'll be fine." Her gaze slid over Nick's cable-knit sweater, jeans and black shoe-boots. "What about you? Are you in Winding Creek for a visit?"

"No. I'm on my way to Cliff Top Ski Lodge. But the snow's getting too deep to get very far until the roads are plowed. Do you know anyone who rents rooms?''

''Yes, but...'' She hesitated for a moment, looking somewhat shy. Then she gave him another one of her smiles. ''I'd be happy to put you up for the night. It's the least I can do to thank you for rescuing Jakie.''

''I can't believe you'd invite me into your home. I'm a stranger!''

She studied him, then shook her head. ''You're not a stranger. Besides the fact we went to the same school for years, I remember one evening when two of the boys on the football team cornered me as I was leaving school after debate practice.''

Unexpectedly, Faith's words took Nick back to a time he'd tried to forget along with everything else about Winding Creek. He could see the instance she'd referred to as if it had happened yesterday. Faith was never considered one of the popular girls, but she was sweet, pretty, and unfortunately in the wrong place at the wrong time and alone that night when two of his teammates were looking for trouble. They'd backed her up against the school building. One had snatched her books. The other was moving in for a stolen kiss when Nick had come upon them, instantly assessing the situation and telling them to back off or he'd make sure they wouldn't play in Saturday's game.

Faith's eyes had still been fearful and glistening with unshed tears when the two football players had swaggered away. She'd thanked Nick as he'd handed her her books. They'd stood there awkwardly for a few moments, neither of them knowing what to say, until two more students had come out of the building. Obviously embarrassed, Faith had thanked him again, then walked with her classmates down the street toward her home. They'd passed each other in the hall the next day, both acting as if the incident had never happened.

Nick's voice was gruff as he said, "I might have done you a favor once, but that doesn't mean I'm safe to invite into your house."

"You rescued me. And now you rescued Jakie. A man who steps in when he doesn't have to isn't the type of man to do us harm." Then she rubbed her arms self-consciously as if she were cold. "But if you'd rather stay somewhere else, that's fine."

There was an uncertainty in Faith's eyes he wanted to wipe away, the same uncertainty he'd seen that night behind the school. Why not accept her hospitality? He'd be on his way in the morning. "I wouldn't rather stay somewhere else. I just don't want to impose on you."

"You won't be," she assured him. "But I should warn you. I have a futon in my office, not an extra bed."

The word "bed" brought pictures to his mind he shouldn't entertain. Especially not with a woman like Faith Hewitt.

When he looked down at her, feeling her kindness, her freshness, the lack of pretense he remembered from their high school years, his heart pounded faster. "A futon is all I need."

Faith's hand trembled as she set the pan of brownies on a cooling rack. She couldn't believe Nicholas Clark was shoveling her front walk! She'd had such a crush on him when she was in high school. Hero worship. Especially after that night he'd rescued her. He'd been so out of reach. At least for her with her shyness, her practical rather than fashionable clothes, her parents who had believed reading and spending time at the library would serve her better than attending parties or dances.

Not that she ever could have gotten close to Nick. He was two years older. He'd run with a different crowd—a faster crowd that did more, knew more and wasn't afraid to take the risk of getting caught with a few beers.

Then a month after graduation, he'd married Pamela Ann Jones—cheerleader, prom queen, most envied young lady in Winding Creek. But the marriage had only lasted a few months and Nick was gone. As far as Faith knew, he'd never returned.

The aroma of brownies filled the small two-story home. Faith lifted the lid on the pot of tomato sauce simmering on the stove. Before she put the spaghetti on to boil, she'd corral Jakie and Nick.

She took her parka from the back of the kitchen chair, zipped it and walked through the living room to the front door. When she stepped onto the porch, she saw it had been shoveled as had the front walk. The short driveway leading to the single car garage bore her Jeep's tracks but was still snow-covered. Nick had followed her home slowly in his sedan, and now it sat blanketed in snow at the curb. Jakie and her houseguest stood on the front walk, snow frosting their coats. Jakie's hat protected him, but although Nick wore a navy down jacket, he stood hatless, the snowflakes falling on his thick black hair.

His shoulders seemed broader than she remembered, the jut of his jaw a little sharper, his lips...

How many times in her fantasies had she thought about kissing Nicholas Clark when she was a teenager...since he'd burst into her life less than two hours ago? She was a mature, responsible woman of twenty-eight who knew better than to dream of a man as attractive and experienced as Nick. She was just so glad she had a chance to pay him back for his kindness so many years ago, let alone for his help today with Jakie.

Pushing the dream out of her mind, she took a deep breath of the slicing cold and went down the steps.

Jakie ran toward her. "Nick shovels fast."

"Nick?" she asked with arched brows. In the six months Jakie had lived with her she'd taught him to address adults respectfully.

"He said I could call him that."

She smiled at the little boy. "Well, then I guess you can. Why don't you go in and get washed up?"

"Okay." Almost before the word was out of his mouth he was running up the steps.

Nick stopped shoveling when he saw her. As her hair blew across her cheek, he stepped closer and the icy temperature seemed much warmer.

"It's time for supper," she said.

"I'd hoped to finish but the way it's still snowing I'll have to do it again later anyway."

"No, you won't. This isn't your responsibility. I'll take care of it tomorrow."

"You don't usually do this yourself, do you?"

The surprise in his voice made her smile. "This is Vermont. I shovel lots of snow. I'm healthy and able-bodied."

He grimaced. "Do I sound like a chauvinist?"

"No. Just a man who might be used to snow blowers or someone else shoveling his walk. Where do you call home now?"

He shrugged and didn't answer for a moment. "I live in Rutland."

"But you're on vacation?" She suddenly wanted to know a lot more about Nick—where he'd been…who he had become.

"If I have to admit it, it's more of an escape than a vacation."

Her silence urged him to say more.

"I've owned a toy store for the past five years. From Thanksgiving till New Year's, it gets crazy. I have capable employees running it, and this year I decided I wanted a quiet Thanksgiving. And actually, I'd just like to skip Christmas."

"Skip Christmas?" she asked as if the thought was incomprehensible.

He shoved one gloved hand into his pocket. "Holidays aren't important to everyone."

"But Christmas…" She stopped when she saw his expression and realized there was another reason Nick wanted to ski rather than just avoiding hustle and bustle. As the snow settled on the top of her nose, she said, "Why don't we talk about this inside."

"There's nothing to talk about," Nick responded. "I'll start the driveway then I'll be in."

His message was clear. They might have passed each other in the school halls, but now they were far removed from each others' lives. Faith left Nick to the shoveling and went inside to put supper on the table.

A short time later, Nick came into the kitchen in his stocking feet. His hair was wind-blown and his beard line made him look rugged and altogether too sexy. He stopped in the doorway and sniffed appreciatively. "Supper smells great."

"I hope you like spaghetti and garlic bread."

"I like almost anything." His gaze drifted over her soft, cream oxford blouse and well-washed jeans, and she wished she'd changed.

Jakie came running in. "I washed, Faith."

"With soap?" she asked.

Nodding, Jakie went to Nick. "You gonna wash up?"

Nick smiled. "I guess I am."

With a matching smile, Jakie grabbed his hand. "C'mon. I'll show you where."

Nick followed the five-year-old through the living room to the bathroom upstairs.

Jakie chattered throughout dinner and slurps of spaghetti, mostly about the pageant. A good listener, Nick asked questions that kept Jakie talking. Faith wondered if he did it so she wouldn't inquire further about his life. After the brownies, which both Jakie and Nick ate with relish, Jakie asked to be excused.

"You can play for a while. But then it's bath time," she reminded him.

"Do I haf to?"

"You know you do. I'll call you when I finish cleaning up."

As Jakie disappeared into the living room, Faith stood and began to clear the table. Suddenly Nick was beside her at the counter with the pan of brownies. He set them down, then touched her shoulder.

Turning, she found him so close she could smell his scent and feel his body heat. She felt such a pull toward him, her eyes mysteriously drawn to his. They were silvery blue and mesmerizing.

"Faith, about what I said when we were outside..."

"I had no right to pry."

"You weren't. It's just that I've tried to forget everything about Winding Creek. Holidays here were…like any other day of the week. If my father wasn't drunk, he was playing poker to try to win rent money. Thanksgiving and Christmas just bring up memories I'd rather forget."

She didn't know what to say. Holidays and family were such an important part of her life, especially Christmas. "Christmas and a toy store seem to go together," she said, curious about him, hoping to get him to reveal more.

Nick looked pensive for a moment. "*Children* and toy stores go together. When I bought the store, I wanted to see kids' faces light up with wonder and excitement and the sheer happiness of playing. Toys help them build and learn and dream. All year-round."

With Winding Creek being a small town, Faith had heard stories about Nick's parents. His mother had left before Nick started school. His father had never gotten over it. They'd lived in a poor section of town where kids ran the streets and teenagers got into trouble. Somehow Nick had risen above all that.

She could see how much owning the toy store meant to him. "I'll bet you let kids try out the toys."

He looked surprised. "Yes, I do. To a certain extent. A corner of the store is filled with samples." He chuckled. "You could say it's a testing area. I find out which ones can withstand a kid's enthusiasm."

"But this year you decided to take a vacation instead of watching?"

The silver left his eyes, leaving them a clear blue. "I haven't taken a vacation since I bought the store five years ago. It was time."

In the silence between them, she could hear the beat of her heart. Nick reached toward her and took the ends of her hair between his fingers, sliding it back and forth. "I can remember sitting behind you at assembly and watching your hair sway across the back of the chair. I always wondered if it was as soft as it looked."

Her hair had been longer then. She remembered the few times he'd sat behind her...how she'd listened to the sound of his deep voice as he talked to friends...how she'd wished she was the type of girl he'd notice. Looking up at him now, she wondered if the years had changed anything.

As Nick bent his head, she thought she might find out. But then she heard the sound of Jakie zooming a truck across the floor in the living room. What was she doing? Trying to live out a teenage fantasy? Taking a deep breath, she backed up.

Nick straightened and stepped away.

The years hadn't changed the fact that she was still a small-town girl and he was the more worldly boy. And now, he didn't even live in Winding Creek. He was just passing through.

Raking his hand though his hair, Nick said, "I'd better finish the driveway. If I get the snow cleared once tonight, there won't be as much to take care of tomorrow."

"If it stops," she murmured, suddenly wishing Nicholas Clark could be snowed in with her forever, yet wondering what she would do with him if he was. What came to mind made her blush.

"It better stop. A pair of skis is waiting for me at Cliff Top," he added, as if he couldn't wait to get there.

She'd better get a grip. Snow or no snow, Nick would be on his way as quickly as he'd arrived. When he went into the living room and picked up his jacket, she realized the crush she'd had on him as a teenager had lain dormant for all these years.

If she knew what was good for her, she'd snuff it out altogether.

After Nick propped the shovel against the front of the house, he shook off his boots and went inside. He'd looked around Faith's house before. But now he took a second, longer look.

He could think of two words to describe Faith's house—homey and comfortable, from the multicolor braided rug to a quilt with patches of every color draped over the back of the slate blue sofa. The sofa itself was made up of pillows across the back and at the arms. The matching chair was huge and looked just as inviting. A wooden rocker sat next to the small brick fireplace with a raised hearth. Against the long wall, an oak entertainment center held a television and compact disc player. Children's videos lined one shelf while photo albums lay on another. Nick suddenly noticed the ivy stenciling around the ceiling, and he bet Faith had stenciled it herself.

After discarding his coat and boots, he went through the living room to the large kitchen. A wrought-iron chandelier hung over the maple table and chairs in the dining area while maple cupboards lined the small kitchen space. When he realized there was nothing but silence downstairs, he climbed the steps in the foyer to the second floor where he'd left his suitcase when he arrived.

A soft, sweet voice drew him toward a small bedroom. A coverlet with cars and trucks in bright primary colors covered the single bed. Goldfish swam in the bowl on the short dresser. But what captivated Nick was the sight of Faith sitting in a platform rocker, singing to and rocking Jakie. The tableau made Nick's heart ache and his chest tighten.

He stood there, silently watching, until Faith must have sensed his presence. She looked up. "He couldn't keep his eyes open tonight for the end of the story."

When she slid forward on the chair, Nick quickly moved into the room and lifted Jakie from her arms. "No point waking him," he murmured. As slight as Faith was, she never could have lifted Jakie from her sitting position to carry him to the bed.

Nick often watched the children who came into his store. But he hadn't held one in his arms for a very long time. He remembered back to a time when he'd thought he'd become a father...the hopes and dreams he'd started weaving. But Pamela Ann had shot those dreams to hell with her lie.

Staring down at Jakie, at the red hair, freckles and innocent face, he envied Faith. He also wondered why she'd never married and how she'd come to be a foster mother to this little boy.

Her arm brushed Nick's as she stood and turned down the bed. Even though the slight contact was simply the cotton of her blouse grazing his sweater, he could feel it through the layer of his shirt and much deeper. Gently he laid Jakie on the bed, then stepped away.

As Nick had always imagined a mother would do, Faith lifted the covers to Jakie's chin, smiled down at him with the most tender look on her face Nick had ever seen and kissed the five-year-old's cheek. Then she brushed his hair across his brow, kissed her fingers and touched them to his forehead. Nick suspected it was a nightly ritual. His chest tightened even more.

Turning away, he left the room and waited for her in the hall.

When she joined him, she left Jakie's door partly open.

"What's his story?" Nick asked, his voice coming out gruffer than he intended.

"Let's go into my office," she suggested, motioning toward the room where he'd left his suitcase.

Touches of homelike warmth found in the rest of the house were also evident in her office, despite the predominance of equipment there—a computer, printer, fax machine, copier, scanner and drafting table. "Nice setup," he remarked.

"It's my work. I develop programs for software companies."

"Working at home has its advantages," Nick said, looking at her now rather than the equipment.

"It sure does. Before Jakie started kindergarten this year, I worked in the mornings before he got up and at night after he went to bed."

Nick leaned against the desk. "Where are his parents?"

"They were killed in a motorcycle accident. He never really knew his father. His mother got pregnant when she was fifteen. Her parents disowned her, but she kept Jakie and moved here about two years ago."

"Did you know her well?" he asked, still trying to figure out Faith's connection.

"I met her at the community center when she needed someone to watch Jakie while she waitressed. She couldn't pay much and I volunteered. It was easy for me to fit my work around her schedule. But when her boyfriend showed up on his Harley, she started to leave Jakie with me more and more. One night, they took a curve too fast and ended up in the wrong lane of traffic. It was a tragic accident that never should have happened."

"He had no relatives?" He couldn't imagine many women taking in a child and all the responsibility it entailed as selflessly as Faith had.

"His mother's family lives in New York. They didn't want responsibility for a child who they felt caused them to lose their daughter. The boy had a father who lives in Texas. He insisted he couldn't care for a child. So that left strangers or me. The authorities let me care for him until I became licensed as an official foster parent, and he's been with me ever since. He's filled an empty place in my heart."

Nick had always guessed Faith was special. Now he knew it. Silence and something electric crackled between them as they stood gazing at each other. Finally, breaking eye contact, she pointed to the single futon that looked like three stacked cushions. "If you unfold that, I'll get you some sheets and towels."

When Faith returned to the room, she set about making up the futon. Nick couldn't keep his eyes off her slender hands, carefully tucking in corners. He stuffed a pillow into a pillowcase, noticing the hand embroidery along the border, smelling the faint flowers of Faith's perfume. They kept bumping into each other, trying to ignore the awkwardness...trying to ignore the chemistry.

When Faith's office phone rang, she had to reach around him to answer it. Her forearm brushed his ribs and he didn't move away immediately until she said a bit breathlessly, "Hello."

Nick automatically wondered who would be calling

her at ten o'clock. A man, perhaps? A woman like Faith certainly had someone special in her life.

"Hi, Mom."

Relief rushed through him, surprising him as much as the pull toward Faith.

"We're fine," she said into the receiver. "Oh, you just heard about it? No, Jakie wasn't scared. In fact, he seemed to enjoy swinging in midair."

Nick continued to watch Faith as she wrapped the phone cord around her little finger and frowned. "Yes, it's true. Nick Clark rescued him."

Something Faith's mother said created a furrow between her brows. He soon surmised what the topic of conversation was.

"After he rescued Jakie and shoveled my walks, the least I could do was offer him a place to stay tonight." Faith glanced at Nick, her cheeks pink.

Her next comment made him realize that Mrs. Hewitt was probably reminding Faith about his reputation as a teenager.

"That was then. This is now. We're adults, Mom. If Mrs. Barley wants to gossip, let her. I'm just being hospitable. Tell Dad to eat plenty of chicken soup. I'm glad his cold's almost gone. I'll try to get over to look at the costumes for the pageant tomorrow. Keep warm. I love you."

After Faith said goodbye and hung up, Nick glanced at his suitcase. "Maybe I'd better find another place to stay. I know how tongues wag in Winding Creek."

Faith waved his suggestion away. "Don't be ridiculous. They'll find something else to talk about tomorrow."

He didn't want her to be the butt of gossip. His reputation in Winding Creek was already set for life; hers should be protected.

Apparently guessing his thoughts and wanting to reassure him, Faith clasped his arm. "You're stranded in Winding Creek and you need a place to sleep. End of story."

He glanced down at her fingers on his arm, enjoyed the heat of her touch and wondered why he felt this wasn't the end of the story, but the beginning. "All right. You win. I really don't want to trek down the street, knocking on doors."

Faith smiled, then dropped her hand and switched her attention to the futon. After a moment of silence, she looked up at him again with soft brown eyes and suggested, "Maybe you should sleep in my bed."

With the circumstances of the day throwing him off-guard, the attraction he felt toward Faith unsettling him, he couldn't help but ask, "With you?"

Chapter Two

Faith's face became a lovely shade of pink. "No, of course not."

He couldn't help moving closer to her, wanting to kiss the flustered shyness in her eyes into desire. "Do you invite many men into your bed?"

"Only when they stay overnight and they're too tall for the futon," she returned with a touch of fire and a bit of wariness that hadn't been evident before.

Smiling, he said, "Sorry. I didn't mean to poke into your personal life."

With the tilt of her head, she studied him. "Yes, you did. But since you probably don't want to tell me about yours, we'll call it a draw." She waved at the futon. "It's going to be short for you and maybe a little narrow. I can sleep in here if you'd prefer my bed."

The idea was tempting. But he'd bet his Christmas profits that her sheets would carry the same scent she wore, and he'd get even less sleep. Besides, a sense of chivalry he hadn't realized he possessed wouldn't let

her give up her comfort for his. "This will be fine. If
you have an extra pillow, I can use it at the foot."

"Be right back," she murmured without meeting his
gaze again.

"Faith?"

She stopped at the door.

"Do you mind if I get a shower?"

"Go ahead. I have some straightening up to do
downstairs. If you need anything, just yell."

From what he'd seen downstairs, everything was as
neat as a pin. Was she nervous about being in close
quarters with him? The thought of her sleeping on the
other side of the wall would be damned intriguing.

When Faith turned away and headed for the stairs,
Nick picked up his towel. The thought was more than
intriguing...it was arousing.

Jakie's call penetrated Nick's sleep. Sitting up, he
heard it again.

"Faith. Faith!"

Nick jumped up and opened the office door in time
to see Faith's nightgown sway around her ankles as she
hurried to the little boy's room. Without thinking about
it, Nick followed her.

She'd already gathered Jakie into her arms and was
rocking and soothing him. "It's okay, honey. I'm right
here. I won't let anything happen to you."

Nick remembered the words—they were the same
ones she'd used as Jakie had swung in the harness.

Tears slipped down Jakie's cheeks. "She went
away."

"I know. But I'm here now, and I love you very
much."

Looking up at Faith with huge blue eyes, Jakie asked, "And you won't *ever* go away?"

Faith hugged him tighter. "Not ever."

For a moment, Nick felt as if he'd been sent back in time. He could feel Jakie's sense of abandonment because he'd experienced it, too. The difference was that his father hadn't known how to comfort a child. He'd been too immersed in his own pain. Thank God Jakie had Faith to rebuild his sense of security.

Nick suddenly felt as if he shouldn't intrude. But Faith gazed at him over the little boy's head. "Jakie had a bad dream."

As Nick sat on the edge of the bed, his bare leg brushed hers under her long pink flannel nightgown. He'd only worn a pair of silk sleeping shorts and was suddenly very aware of how they were both dressed.

Focusing his attention on the child in her arms, he said, "The good thing about bad dreams is that they disappear when you open your eyes."

From the shelter of Faith's arms, Jakie asked, "Do *you* have bad dreams?"

"Not so much anymore. But I did. When I was your age and even older."

"Jakie and I have talked about why we have bad dreams...that it's our heart and mind's way of helping us with sad and angry feelings."

Faith Hewitt was a wise woman and because he, himself, felt so in tune with Jakie, Nick wanted to help him. Picking up the stuffed bear that lay by the pillow, Nick sat the bear on his lap. "I used to have a toy dog that was my very best friend. I told him all about my dreams—the bad ones *and* the good ones."

Jakie sat up in Faith's arms and reached for the bear. "I talk to Teddy. After Faith turns the light off."

"Bears and dogs listen very carefully," Nick said seriously.

Jakie nodded then gave a huge yawn.

"You'd better get back to sleep," Nick suggested.

"Can I help shovel again tomorrow?" Jakie asked him.

"Sure." Standing, he patted Jakie's leg. "I'll see you in the morning."

Trying to ignore the feelings the scene in Jakie's room stirred up, Nick returned to the office and repositioned the two pillows Faith had deposited in his room earlier while he was taking a shower. He'd listened for her footsteps after he'd settled in for the night, but had fallen asleep without hearing them.

"Nick, I'm sorry we woke you."

She stood in his doorway, a vision in pink flannel, her sweet scent even stronger now than earlier in the day. He suspected it was lotion rather than perfume. Her hair was tousled.

"Does he wake up often?"

"Less now than at the beginning."

No matter how hard Nick tried, he couldn't keep his distance from Faith. When he approached her, her gaze swept over his bare chest, then to the silk shorts. If she kept looking at him like that, there'd be more to see.

She must have realized she'd been staring because she lifted her gaze to his, her cheeks flushed. "Are you comfortable in here?"

"I must be. I fell asleep before you came up."

Needing to feel the silkiness of her hair again, wanting to touch the softness of her skin, he slid his thumb along her cheek and brushed her hair away from her face. "Mothering comes naturally to you."

"I love Jakie," she murmured, lowering her gaze.

He knew why she was afraid to look at him, but he lifted her chin with his knuckle so she had no choice. When her eyes met his, he could see the desire sparkling there…the curiosity about what could happen next. It was time they found out.

When he slid his arm around her, she didn't back away. She simply gazed up at him with the same excited anticipation he was experiencing. In his thirty years, he'd never analyzed kissing; he'd just done it. But this time, he intended to savor every moment of it, not considering the kiss simply as a means to an end.

As he took a deep breath to take in more of Faith's scent, he studied her face, her honey lashes, the few freckles along her nose. He pulled her closer slowly, bending his head, only closing his eyes when his lips touched hers.

He heard her soft sigh, felt the tremulous quiver of her lower lip. But when he increased the pressure, she responded by lifting her hands to his shoulders.

The heat from her fingertips scorched him and he wanted more of it. He slid his tongue along the seam of her lips, back and forth, until she opened to him. When she did, he moved his hands to the small of her back and pressed her closer as he tasted her. She was velvet and intoxicating and a gift he'd never expected.

Until abruptly she pushed against his chest and wrenched away.

Releasing her, he tried to rein in the desire racing through him. "What's wrong?"

"*That* was wrong. I'm not one of the cheerleaders you dated in high school!"

"Thank goodness." He couldn't keep the amusement from his voice.

"I'm serious, Nick. You didn't take a second look at me then and I wonder why you are now. Because I'm in the same house and available?"

Whew! The kiss had apparently fueled more anger than desire. "Wait a minute." He held her shoulders so she wouldn't turn away. "What makes you think I didn't take a second look?"

"Don't snow me, Nick. I didn't run around in your crowd. I didn't run in *any* crowd. I was a nerd. I wore long skirts and I studied. The only thing I was missing was braces."

"And glasses," he reminded her while she was on a roll. "Because despite what you think I *did* give you a second look...and a third—in the cafeteria, winning awards as a member of the debate team, writing articles for the school paper."

"Nick, you can't tell me you were ever interested..."

"I wasn't good enough for you."

Her mouth rounded in surprise. "What?"

"You came from a good family and a nice part of town."

"So did Pamela Ann," she returned quickly, obviously not believing him.

Nick still felt resentment toward his ex-wife. "Pam wasn't like you. She was as wild as I was and used any means she could—" He stopped, not wanting to get into his brief marriage and its abrupt end. Taking Faith's chin in his hand, he said, "I respected you...your youth, your innocence. You weren't the type of girl I *could* date."

There was still confusion in her eyes.

"*I* had to *become* respectable, Faith."

"Oh, Nick," she sighed as she covered his hand

with hers. "You always *were* respectable. You just didn't know it."

Never had he wanted to kiss a woman the way he wanted to kiss Faith again. But he wouldn't take advantage of her or spending the night under her roof. Pulling his hand from under hers, he put a good foot between them. "You'd better go to your room."

She folded her hands in front of her. "Would you like me to wake you up in the morning?"

"I have an alarm on my watch. I set it for seven."

"If it keeps snowing, the mountain roads won't be open."

"I'll play it by ear."

The awkwardness between them was almost as tangible as the sparks. Finally Faith said, "I'll see you in the morning.

He nodded.

When she closed his door behind her, he breathed a sigh of relief. After he switched off the light, he settled on the futon in the dark, trying to think about his upcoming vacation. But as he closed his eyes, all he saw was Faith rocking Jakie.

Faith trudged beside Nick in the snow while he carried Jakie on his shoulders. Electricity was out on the north end of town where the schools were located and they'd been closed. Fortunately the residential sections still had power. The roads were closed, too, so Nick really had no choice but to stay in Winding Creek. He didn't seem overjoyed but he didn't seem upset, either. After last night's kiss, they'd kept their distance this morning at breakfast. He'd shoveled more snow, then she'd suggested a walk to the community center. She had to get to work on the scenery, and she knew any volunteers within walking distance would be there, too. She hoped so. Because it wouldn't be a good idea for her and Nick to spend much time together without other adults present.

Stuffing her mittened hands into her pockets, she remembered Nick holding her in his arms all too vividly. And the kiss...the first brush of his lips, his tongue exciting her, his hands pressing her closer. She glanced at him and saw him looking at the houses and stores along Main Street as if he was seeing them for the first time.

Nick opened the door to the community center for Faith. As she preceded him inside, her arm brushed his companionably, yet the feelings from being close to him were much more than companionable. Once inside, Jakie saw one of his friends and waved and squiggled until Nick set him on the floor. Other members of the community waved and called greetings to Faith, giving her the sense of community she so loved about Winding Creek.

One of the men at the front of the room, who'd been packing canned goods into boxes for the annual Thanksgiving food drive, separated himself from the group and came toward them with a huge grin.

Bud Matson was almost as tall as Nick, with the same football player's broad shoulders. His brown hair and mustache were salted with premature gray. He clapped Nick on the shoulder. "Is that you, Nick? My gosh, it's been years!"

Nick smiled. "It sure has. But you're looking good."

Bud grimaced and patted his thickened midsection. "Not as fit as I used to be, but I can't complain. Margie feeds me too well."

"Margie Cromwell?" Nick guessed.

"She's been Margie Matson for over nine years. Faith, here, can attest that she keeps me on the straight and narrow," he joked.

Margie had been in Faith's class in high school and Bud had been in Nick's. "How's Margie feeling?" Faith asked.

Bud shook his head. "The last month is always the hardest for her. She just wants the baby to come." To Nick, he said, "We have eight-year-old twins who are at home with Margie, and George over there who's Jakie's age. This one will be our fourth."

Faith watched Nick's expression become a little more set and she wondered what he was thinking. But he simply said to his old friend, "Congratulations. Tell Margie I said hello."

"You should stop in. How long are you going to be in town?"

"Just until the roads clear. I'm only passing through."

Bud studied Nick for a moment. "You know, Pamela Ann left Winding Creek not long after you two split. Something about a modeling career in New York. I've heard she's been in some mail-order catalogues."

If Nick's expression had been set before, now it became downright stoney. "We didn't keep in touch."

Faith had so many questions she wanted to ask Nick about his short marriage. In fact...she didn't even know if he was married or involved with someone now! And she'd kissed the man. He didn't wear a ring, but some married men didn't. He could be meeting someone at Cliff Top... Suddenly horrified she might have done something diametrically opposed to her values, she felt her cheeks get hot.

Bud took Nick's short answer in stride. "Well, if you do stick around a few days, we'll have to go out some night and rehash old times and football plays. Did you come in here today to help with the packing and sorting?"

"Whatever needs to be done," Nick answered.

Bud motioned to the stacks of food and boxes. "Take off your coat and I'll show you what we're doing."

As Bud moved away, Nick shrugged out of his jacket. "I guess the snow has shut down quite a few businesses."

Faith knew Nick was referring to a half dozen men working with items for the food drive. "Bud teaches at the high school and coaches. Most of the other men are teachers, too. With school closed today, they're available."

When Nick would have followed Bud, Faith caught his arm. "I have to ask you something."

The seriousness of her tone stopped him as much as the pressure of her hand. "What?"

She didn't know any other way to ask except by blurting it out. "Are you married...or involved with anyone?"

His arm stiffened under her fingers. "Do you think I would have kissed you last night if I was?"

His probing blue eyes made her terribly uncomfortable, but she had to be honest. "I don't know."

There was an edge of anger in his voice when he responded. "No, I'm not married. I'm not involved. I know the meaning of a promise, Faith. And I know what's right and wrong."

With that, he pulled away from her grasp and she realized she'd insulted him. Last night she'd told him she'd always considered him "respectable." But her question just now had made her look like a hypocrite. She owed him an apology, but she wasn't sure he'd accept it.

She'd kept her eye on Jakie while they were talking. He was playing with Bud's son at one of the tables, building a miniature city with blocks. Pulling a clipboard from her carryall, Faith made sure she had a few pieces of graph paper and headed for the stage determined to apologize to Nick later. She reminded herself why she'd come today—to get started on the set design for the pageant. The script required two separate scene settings. The children would be portraying the Christmas story within a contemporary plot about a little boy who finds the meaning of Christmas in giving his smiles and time to his grandfather rather than receiving presents.

Standing by the side of the stage, Faith sketched, then crumpled and tossed ideas, keeping track of Jakie, glancing now and then at Nick. Finally, with a sigh, she ran her fingers through her hair.

"Problem?" A deep male voice asked at her shoulder.

She spun around. "Nick. About what I asked you earlier...I'm sorry—"

"There's nothing to be sorry about. You don't know me well enough to know how I live my life." He pointed to the waste can where she'd tossed discarded sketches. "None of your ideas working?"

He obviously wanted to close the subject, and there was really nothing more she could say. "Um, it's a little difficult to plan scenery on cardboard panels."

"Why cardboard? Why not plywood?"

"It's more expensive. We'd need saws and the expertise in using them. The center has a very low budget for the pageant. We'd rather spend the money on families who need help."

Nick got a very intent expression on his face. But before he voiced his thoughts, Bud called to them. "Nick. Faith. Come have some lunch. Mrs. Barley brought a whole box of sandwiches and bags of potato chips. Water's on for hot chocolate, coffee, or tea."

"I'd forgotten how everyone in this town pitches in," Nick murmured.

"What *do* you remember?" Faith asked softly.

The lines around his eyes deepened and the nerve in his jaw worked. "I remember being dirt poor and acting like I wasn't. I remember the citizens of this town calling my father a bum when they'd had no idea what he'd been through or what made him drink. When my mother left, it tore out his insides and he had nothing left. Do-gooders condemned him but didn't help him. That's what I remember about Winding Creek."

Finally Faith understood better why Nick had left and why he didn't want to stay any longer than he had to. "Where's your father now?"

Nick probed her gaze for a long time. She guessed he was looking for curiosity rather than genuine concern. But he must have found concern because he answered her. "He's in Florida. Wandering, but sober. At least he was the last time I spoke with him. He works on boats, refinishing them, doing engine work. But I never know where to find him until he calls me."

"It sounds as if you get along."

"We always have. I understand him. I admire the way he turned his life around after he left here, soon after I did."

Faith was curious about Nick's life since he'd left

the small town, but she suspected she'd pushed the personal questions far enough. "We'd better get some lunch. Jakie's already headed for the potato chips."

"I'm going to take a walk. You go ahead."

The snow had still been falling lightly when they entered the building, and she hated the fact that Nick would rather be out in the cold than inside the community center. "These are good people, Nick. They won't treat you like an outcast."

He reached out and touched her cheek gently, as if thanking her for her concern. "Maybe not. But I need some fresh air. You'll be here a while?"

The warmth of his thumb on her cheek sent tingles down her spine. Somehow she found her voice. "We'll stay until Jakie gets tired or until I come up with a set design. But don't worry about us. We know our way home."

Nick gave her a small smile. "I have no doubts about that. I'll see you later."

Faith watched Nick stop and say a few words to Jakie. The five-year-old grinned and nodded. Then Nick zippered his coat and left the community center. Faith wasn't at all sure he'd come back.

Children played in the snow along the street, towing sleds behind them, stooping to pack and throw snowballs at each other. But Nick didn't stop to watch. He kept walking. Ever since he'd stopped his car in Winding Creek, he'd felt unsettled. His attraction to Faith didn't help, nor did their conversation. He didn't talk about the past. He certainly had never confided his feelings about it to anyone. Yet he'd done both with Faith. Why?

Because, back here once again, he had to put all of it to rest.

Unshoveled walks slowed Nick's progress as he trudged through the snow to the south side of town. The railroad tracks were hidden under the ten inches of snow that had fallen since yesterday, but the railroad crossing sign marked the division of the more prosperous part of Winding Creek and his old neighborhood.

He hadn't walked very far when he realized the area he'd intended to revisit had changed. Old brick houses had been sandblasted and repointed. Brand-new storm doors hung on the row of homes. The biggest surprise of all came when he reached the corner. No white clapboard run-down structure stood there. It was gone, along with the apartment where he'd grown up, the scarred lopsided shutters, the tilted chimney. A spic-and-span clean corner grocery store had replaced it.

The change was a blow Nick had to absorb.

He checked the street sign.

Yep, this was the right corner.

But everything he'd known had been wiped away…as if he'd never lived there.

Nicholas Clark might have lived in any other place, in any other part of the United States. He felt adrift, as if an hour ago he'd known his roots and now he didn't.

Faith had spoken of going home. His apartment over the store back in Rutland wasn't a home. It was a place where he ate and slept and worked. This had been his home.

Nick was suddenly gripped by the desire to leave something concrete of himself in Winding Creek, to make a mark somehow. If he stayed a few more days, he could build that scenery for the community center. They might not have a budget that would accommodate plywood and a saw, but he did. He could put some of his old construction skills to work.

And when he left, he'd leave something behind, something that would be used and noticed at least for one night and, if he used his ingenuity, maybe for years to come.

Now all he had to do was see if the hardware store was open.

Jakie and George—who looked more like Bud everyday—crawled in and out of a refrigerator carton someone had brought in to use as a backdrop. Faith had finally come up with a few sketches, but she wasn't satisfied with the results.

As she went to the urn in the corner to get hot water for a cup of tea, the community center door flew open. Nick walked in, a huge box in his arms, followed by two teenagers carrying sheets of plywood and two more who were lugging studs.

Faith set down her cup and hurried to him. "What's all this?"

Nick motioned the teenage boys to the stage. "Over there. In the back."

He set the box on the table and pulled open the flaps. "I decided to stay a few days, maybe until after Thanksgiving, and build you a set that will do your pageant proud."

"But, Nick, I told you we can't afford—"

Lifting the saw from the box, he smiled. "The center doesn't have to pay for anything. I'm donating the material and the saw and the labor. Anyone who wants to help me is welcome to."

Faith didn't know what had happened on Nick's walk or why he'd decided to stay. But she was pleased and couldn't keep the joy from filling her heart. "You know how to build a set?" she teased.

"I worked on construction crews in high school and afterward."

"Before the toy store?"

"Before the toy store. The money was good. It was a means to an end. When I had enough saved for a down payment, I invested in a business. Now let me show you what I have in mind." He took a folded sheet of paper from his jacket pocket.

She stepped closer to him so she could see and breathed in the scent of soap and slight spice mixed with cold air. When he pointed to the diagram he'd sketched, she realized his palm was almost twice the size of hers.

"This is a unit with three panels nailed together on a base with wheels," he explained. "I'll build three of them and they'll line the back of the stage. You'll be able to have three separate backdrops and between scenes, anyone can roll them into the right position."

"What a terrific idea! I can already envision three scenes for the panels. I'll just explain them to Margie and she can sketch them on. I don't know how to thank you."

He clasped her shoulder. "I'm not just doing this for the center, Faith. I'm doing it for me, too. It's hard to explain."

By returning to Winding Creek, even under protest, Nick had apparently made peace with something in his past...or was trying to. "You don't have to explain."

His gaze held hers, and the heat in it should have melted her on the spot. An invisible bond of understanding pulled them closer together until the noises around them faded away.

"I need to ask you something, Faith," he said, his voice husky. "And I want you to be straight with me."

She nodded. "I will."

"Do you want me to find another place to stay?"

Chapter Three

Faith examined her heart carefully before she answered. If Nick stayed with her, he might kiss her again. And if he kissed her again...

She was still a small-town girl without the flash of the women he probably dated. And he would be moving on. If only she could remember both those facts when he looked at her...when he touched her.

Making a decision, she told herself she *could* remember them, and she wouldn't lose her heart in a few days. Nick was a friend who needed a place to stay and she could provide it. He was waiting for her answer. "You're welcome to stay with Jakie and me as long as you'd like. We'd enjoy having you with us for Thanksgiving."

Instead of the smile she expected, he frowned. "You'll let me pay you?"

"Of course not!"

"Faith, if I stayed in a motel..."

"There are no motels in Winding Creek."

His frown became a reprimanding scowl. "You know what I mean."

"Yes, and I also know spending a few nights on my futon doesn't require payment."

"Stubborn, aren't you?"

"No. Hospitable. And it will be good for Jakie to have a male influence for a little while. That is, if you don't mind—"

Nick's face got a tender, pleased look. "I don't mind. Jakie's a great kid. But if you won't let me pay for my space on your futon, I insist on taking you grocery shopping."

"I'm cooking on Thanksgiving so Mom doesn't have to. I can't expect you to—"

"Great. I like leftovers so I'll pick out the biggest turkey." At her hesitation, he said, "Let me do this, Faith. I don't like to owe anyone."

Nick was a proud man and she did want him to stay. "All right. I'll let you pay for the groceries," she agreed.

At her acquiescence, he smiled. "Good. Now come up on the stage with me and we'll discuss the exact size of the set."

For the next hour or so, Nick began working on the three mobile units while Jakie watched at a safe distance and Faith planned the three scenes for the panels. She was sitting on the edge of the stage when she heard the telephone ring in the kitchen. A few moments later Bud called to her. "It's your mom."

From his position at a sawhorse where he'd placed a sheet of plywood for cutting, Nick said, "Go ahead. I'll keep an eye on Jakie."

Faith jumped the two feet to the floor and hurried to the kitchen. "Hi, Mom. What's up?"

"Would you and Jakie like to come for supper? Your father's feeling better and he's getting restless. I won't let him go out and run the snow blower. Mr. Goldstein did it for us this morning and I baked him a pie. So your father's a bit grumpy."

Faith smiled. Although her father had retired last year, he tried to keep busy. Inactivity did make him grumpy. "We'd like to come, but we still have a guest. Nick will be staying in Winding Creek a few days."

Stark silence lasted at least thirty seconds until Faith's mother asked, "With you?"

"Yes."

"What are you thinking of, Faith? It's improper having a man at your house. And Nicholas Clark, no less."

"He needs a place to stay because he's helping with the set for the pageant."

"I don't understand it, Faith. If the man was simply passing through, why has he decided to stay?"

"It really doesn't matter, Mom."

"It does if he gets fresh with you!"

"Mother..."

"I don't like it."

"You don't know Nick, Mom."

"And you didn't, either, before yesterday. Unless you snuck out behind our backs when you were in high school. Did you?"

"Of course not, Mom. And I can't let Nick sit alone at my house while Jakie and I come to dinner."

After a long pause, her mother sighed loud enough for her to hear. "Bring along your houseguest. Maybe I can convince him to stay here instead."

"I want Nick to stay with me. He'll be good for Jakie. Please don't interfere."

Silence again, until her mother gave in. "All right.

I won't. But if I see you headed for trouble, I won't hold my tongue."

"I know you won't, Mom. I'll see you this evening around six."

After Faith hung up the phone, she wondered if she should have declined the invitation. But since her parents would be coming to dinner on Thursday, Nick might as well meet them tonight. That is if he even wanted to go.

If he didn't, she'd have two days to prepare him for her mother's old-fashioned and inquisitive nature.

Nick thought Faith seemed uncomfortable as she stood beside him in the foyer of the house where she'd grown up. Her mother had arched her brows when she'd seen Jakie's hand nestled in Nick's large one. He had been surprised when the five-year-old had taken his hand outside the front door. It had filled him with a warm feeling he'd never experienced before.

But now Jakie was excited. He unzipped his insulated jacket and squiggled out of it, sat on the floor and took off his shoe-boots, then announced, "I'm gonna find Grandpa Hewitt."

"He's downstairs working on his ducks. You be careful on the stairs," Faith's mother warned.

"My father carves duck decoys," Faith explained to Nick.

Constance Hewitt took Nick's coat and hung it in the foyer closet. After she hung Faith's and Jakie's beside it, she turned to Nick. "Well, Nicholas, it's been years since I heard you got a divorce and left town. What are you doing these days?"

Although Faith had warned Nick that her mother didn't believe any question was off-limits, he hadn't expected an inquisition as soon as he stepped in the door. But then he saw the concerned look on Constance's face and the troubled one on Faith's. Apparently more had passed between mother and daughter other than the simple invitation to dinner and its acceptance.

"I own a toy store now in Rutland, Mrs. Hewitt, and I'm thinking about opening another."

"How interesting. I hear toy stores are doing quite well."

"Businesses with a good foundation that are managed well usually do," he said without telling her specifically what she wanted to hear.

"And you find you can take a vacation at what must be the busiest time of your year?"

"Mother, I don't think that's any of our business."

"Nonsense, Faith, it's just a general question," her mother protested. "I'm curious."

Nick had the sudden urge to put his arm around Faith and assure her she didn't have to act as a buffer. "I have an excellent manager who can handle the day-to-day routine as well as I can, even at Christmas. He knows where he can reach me if he needs me." He'd called Greg Blumfield and given him the number this afternoon after he'd decided to stay a few days.

"It's fortunate you have someone you can trust." Constance motioned to the living room. "Make yourself comfortable. I'll go pry Tom away from his ducks. Faith, maybe after dinner you could look at the costumes I'm working on. I found robes for the wise men but I need you to check the sizes for the angels."

As Constance went through the dining room into the kitchen, Nick sat on the sofa. He had to smile when Faith chose the rocker opposite him. "Are you afraid your mother will scold you if you sit beside me?"

When Faith blushed, he chuckled. "Sorry. I couldn't resist."

"No, *I'm* sorry for the grilling. She..."

"She remembers my reputation, knows my background and disapproves of my staying with you. She's a mother, Faith. What else would you expect?"

Faith's brown eyes met his squarely. "I expect her to trust my judgment and accept my friends."

Somehow, in an incredibly short time, he and Faith had developed a bond. It wasn't logical, but he felt closer to her than he'd felt to anyone in years. "Are we friends?"

She tilted her head and smiled. "I think so."

Before Nick could admit to himself his feelings for Faith were more than merely friendly, Jakie ran into the room, a small duck decoy in his hand. He held it up for Faith to see. "Grandpa Hewitt said I can have this."

Faith's father followed Jakie into the living room. His hair, once brown, was gray and receding.

"That one is one of a kind. I thought Jakie could keep it in his room," he explained as Faith examined the small decoy. Then he extended his hand to Nick. "It's good to see you again."

Nick couldn't find censure in Tom Hewitt's eyes. They were the same dark brown as Faith's...clear and welcoming. "It was kind of you and your wife to invite me to dinner."

Tom chuckled. "I'm not sure 'kind' has anything to do with it. Connie just wants to keep an eye on you and my daughter. Me...I figure Faith's grown-up and can handle her life very well." He patted Jakie's head. "After all, look at the wonderful gift she's brought us."

Faith gazed up at her father with the love and admiration Nick would like to see in his own child's eyes someday. And when she put her arms around Jakie and gave him a hug, Nick could see the child was the center of her world. The longing to be a member of that type of family unit shook Nick, and his life back in Rutland seemed empty in comparison.

The lingering smell of roast beef still wafted through the house, although Faith had helped her mother put the leftovers away. Jakie was showing Nick her father's duck decoys in the basement so she'd taken the opportunity to come upstairs.

The white muslin angel costumes hung on a tailor's rack in her mother's sewing room. Constance Hewitt was an excellent seamstress. She'd made most of Faith's clothes throughout her school years. They'd been beautifully sewn, but conservative, sometimes making Faith wish she could have bought from the flamboyant clothes racks at the department stores in Burlington, only a half hour away. But then she'd felt guilty for thinking it.

The angel robes were just the right sizes for the five children who would be dressed in them. She'd help her mother make the wings soon. Leaving the sewing room, Faith peeked into the bedroom that used to be hers. She'd taken most of her belongings to her house when she'd bought it. But her mother had seemed to want to keep a few mementoes—a favorite doll with a full petticoat and pink taffeta dress, a set of teenage mystery novels and one of Faith's yearbooks. She pulled it from the white bookshelves. It was her sophomore yearbook and it would include Nick's senior picture.

Nick.

He'd handled supper well, keeping conversation on the changes that had occurred in Winding Creek, her father's retirement and his new hobby. As Jakie chattered about watching Nick build scenery, her mother had been too distracted to ask more personal questions.

Opening the yearbook, Faith turned to the senior pictures. Nick was easy to find. His hair was longer back then, but his eyes were just as intense, his jaw just as chiseled. He looked more ruggedly handsome now. Only one phrase ran under his picture and name—Football team.

"This was your room?" Nick asked from the doorway.

Faith quickly closed the yearbook and held it by her side, feeling like that teenager again who'd had a crush on someone out of her reach. "Mmm-hmm."

With a smile he came into the room and lifted the yearbook from her hand. But he didn't open it to his picture. He paged through until he found hers. She grabbed for the book, but with a laugh he held it high out of her reach.

"C'mon now. Let me take a look," he teased.

His eyes were twinkling, his voice was gentle, and she couldn't resist the charm of his smile. "You have ten seconds and then we close it permanently," she agreed with a frown.

His amusement evident, he found the page again easily. "I don't know why you're embarrassed. You've hardly changed."

"I looked so...so..."

"Young?" he supplied with another of those smiles that could melt her at his feet.

"Backward," she confessed, knowing her color was much too high.

He closed the book and slid it onto the bookshelf with the other books. Then he turned to her, and they were standing very close. "Maybe you thought of yourself that way, but others didn't see you that way."

"You're being kind."

"I'm being honest."

She gazed over his shoulder out the window, even though she couldn't see anything but darkness through the frosted pane. "Even in college, it was the same."

Cupping her chin, he made her face him. "What *it* was the same?"

"Dating. Boys."

"One boy in particular?"

"Nick…"

"Tell me," he demanded with gentle authority that convinced her he wanted to hear.

She straightened her shoulders and told him very matter-of-factly, "I didn't go to frat parties because I spent most of my time in the computer lab. I met someone there. I thought I'd fallen in love. Unfortunately, it turned out he wanted my programming skills and ideas for a paper he was working on rather than a long-term relationship."

Nick's frown was as grim as his tone. "He used you."

"Yes."

"You haven't been involved with anyone since?"

She shook her head, still feeling naive, gullible and much too vulnerable.

"You don't know your own worth," Nick murmured as he bent his head and slipped his hand under her hair.

An instant later, the demanding pressure of his lips proclaimed louder than any words that he desired her as a woman. As his hand stroked her hair, she felt beautiful. When his tongue thrust into her mouth, she responded freely, forgetting about the girl she used to be in favor of remembering Nick's first kiss, and getting lost in the second one.

She gripped Nick's shoulders, taut and muscled under his sweater, leaned closer into him—

"Oh, my!"

Constance Hewitt's voice pierced the room, dousing their desire.

Nick ended the kiss and lifted his head. Faith jerked away, breathless, and wondering how in the world she was going to explain.

"Faith, what's going on?" her mother asked.

Before Faith could form a response, Nick stepped forward. "We haven't done anything wrong, Mrs. Hewitt."

"You have no right to take advantage of her. Especially not in my home..."

"He wasn't taking advantage of me, Mom."

"I hate to think what's happening at your house," her mother went on as if Faith hadn't spoken. "And with Jakie there. Honestly, Faith, I expect better of you—"

"Stop it, Mom," Faith demanded, her cheeks still hot. "I have always done what you expected. What *I* expected. What happens between Nick and me is no one's business but ours. I'm sorry if we overstepped your bounds of discretion. We'll make sure it doesn't happen again."

She slipped in front of Nick to the doorway where her mother stood, looking stunned Faith would dare talk to her like an independent woman rather than a daughter. Changing the subject, trying to find her equilibrium again, she said, "The costumes look terrific. This is going to be the center's best pageant to date. But now I think I'd better take Jakie home. It's getting late and he'll probably have school tomorrow."

After a look over her shoulder at Nick and his serious expression, she took her mother's arm, and guided her toward the staircase. "Have you decided yet what you're getting Daddy for Christmas?"

"Faith, I think we should talk about..."

"I made him a pair of argyle socks. Is there something else he'd *really* like to have?"

As the women's voices faded away, Nick stuffed his hands into his pockets. He'd never meant to put Faith in an awkward position with her own family. But to his surprise and dismay, he couldn't seem to keep his distance. He couldn't seem to keep himself from wanting more than he should ever think about taking. This attraction to Faith made no sense!

Finally admitting to himself he was staying in Winding Creek as much to spend more time with Faith as to build a stage set, he realized he'd felt more protective of her after that kiss than he'd ever felt about anyone. It was almost as if he'd worn blinders since his marriage to Pamela Ann...almost as if he'd guarded his heart from feeling all these years. And now...

Now he didn't know what the hell he was doing, acting on instinct, maybe treading into territory he should stay clear of.

But when he was with Faith, his restlessness eased. He felt connected to someone. The need to lose himself in work vanished. The problem was that he needed to remind himself about the consequences of feeling again…and remember the difference between his roots in Winding Creek and Faith's.

Back at Faith's house a short time later, Nick switched on the television while she put Jakie to bed. She hadn't looked him in the eye since their encounter with her mother. Mrs. Hewitt's gaze had been cold when she'd said good-night, and he bet she'd have another discussion with her daughter about the kiss she'd witnessed.

Nick was surfing through the channels when Faith called down the stairs. "Nick? Jakie wants to ask you something. Can you come up?"

Nick climbed the steps and went to Jakie's room. The five-year-old smiled and looked up at him expectantly. "Can you cut down a Christmas tree with me…and the other kids…and their dads?"

Beside Jakie on the bed, Faith explained further. "It's become a tradition every year on the Saturday after Thanksgiving for the kindergarten children and their fathers to ride out to Walker's Woods and cut down a Christmas tree for the school lobby. The first-through fourth-graders make ornaments, the fifth- and sixth-graders string popcorn."

"I see," Nick said because he wasn't sure what to say.

"Faith says Saturday is four days away." He held up four fingers. "Will you still be here?"

Jakie wanted him to be a surrogate father. That was a big responsibility. But he couldn't disappoint this little boy who touched a chord in him that had been silent for years. "I'll make sure I'm still here. I've never gone to the woods to cut down a Christmas tree."

Jakie hopped out of bed and hugged Nick around the

waist. Nick's eyes burned as he looked down at the little boy and returned the hug. After he wished the child good dreams and saw him settled in bed once again, he went to Faith's office. That morning he'd expected to sleep here one more night. Now, he might possibly be here through the weekend. His heart felt lighter than it had in years. It was simply a much-needed change of scene. It was simply...

Faith appeared at the door. "Are you going to turn in now?"

He looked around her office and realized she might need to use it. "That depends. Did you want to work?"

"It can wait till morning."

"Faith, if you want to work, I can watch TV. I don't mind." Already, he'd figured out Faith was a people-pleaser and put her needs behind everyone else's.

"I would like to for a while. I'm working on a project that has to be mailed on Friday. I should be able to finish it up tomorrow."

"What kind of project?"

"Software for the family budget and investments. The company I'm working with wants to give the front-runner serious competition."

Stepping through the doorway, Nick motioned her inside. "It's all yours. If it gets late, I can sleep on the sofa."

"I'll be finished before midnight. I want to start fresh again in the morning while Jakie's at kindergarten."

She would have slipped by him without touching him but he couldn't let her do that. He cupped her elbow. "We didn't talk about what happened at your parents'."

"There's nothing to talk about," she said softly.

"I'm sure your mother doesn't feel that way."

Faith shook her head. "My mother still sees me as a little girl rather than an adult. She also thinks men should still kiss women on the hand rather than the lips."

Nick laughed. "You aren't serious."

Faith gave him a wry smile. "Almost."

As they gazed at each other, both of their smiles slid away and Nick wondered if she was remembering the kiss as vividly as he was. The sparks that had danced between them since he'd seen Faith again at the community center crackled in the small space between them.

Releasing her elbow, he dropped his hand to his side. "You'd better get to work and I'd better go downstairs before we're sidetracked into something that could get a lot more complicated than a kiss."

Then he turned away before he took her in his arms and acted like her lover rather than a houseguest.

When the doorbell rang late Wednesday afternoon, Faith shut down her computer. She'd finally finished her project. Her mother had picked up Jakie and taken him with her, insisting he could help make his angel wings. Her mother loved spending time with Jakie, but Faith suspected she'd also wanted to check on what she and Nick were or weren't doing. No problem there. She hadn't seen Nick since breakfast. He'd left for the center, and she guessed he wanted to finish the work on the set so he could leave as soon as he completed it.

Hurrying down the steps, she remembered Nick's expression when Jakie had asked him essentially to be his dad for a day. He'd looked so pleased...so honored.

Faith opened her door and smiled when she recognized the woman standing there. Darla Granger, a woman in her mid-forties, always in a hurry, was Jakie's caseworker and had done everything in her power to help Faith get Jakie settled in her care quickly with the least amount of hassle.

When Faith invited Darla inside, she could tell there was a purposeful air about her that said she'd come for a specific reason. "Come in. Jakie's with my mom this afternoon. He should be back shortly. Would you like a cup of tea?"

Darla shook her head. "I don't have time. I'm already late for an appointment."

A kernel of concern developed in Faith. "How can I help you?"

Darla didn't even unbutton her coat. "There's a couple who wants to adopt Jakie."

Faith's heart almost stopped.

"They want to meet him and I'd like to set it up for Friday. Is that all right with you?"

"Friday?" So many emotions tumbled over one another in Faith that she couldn't sort them.

"Yes. The Brewers want a child as soon as possible and when they saw Jakie's picture and read his history, they were sure he's the one. But of course they'd like to spend a little time with him before we start the official paperwork. Will Friday afternoon suit you for the first meeting?"

Faith felt so cold...numb. Jakie would be part of a family. She'd never expected this to happen so soon. She'd never expected this to happen at all. They'd settled into a life...

"Faith? My appointment's in Burlington and I have to get going. Will you be home on Friday afternoon?"

Automatically Faith answered. "Yes, we'll be here. But you're not going to take Jakie anytime soon, are you?"

"Faith, you knew his placement with you was only temporary. My goal is to see him permanently established in the right situation. The Brewers can provide that. And if Jakie gets along with them, permanent placement could happen quickly." Darla patted Faith's arm. "This is the kind of couple I always hope will adopt. You have a happy Thanksgiving. I'll see you on Friday."

Faith felt frozen as she closed the door behind Darla, then she mechanically went to the kitchen to make herself a cup of tea. She didn't know what else to do. She suddenly felt as if the bottom had dropped out of her world.

Fifteen minutes later, the cup of tea sat in front of her at the table, the tea bag still steeping. When she heard the front door open, the sound broke her trance. But she saw it was Nick, not Jakie and her mother, so she didn't get up.

Nick entered the kitchen with a smile of satisfaction. "One unit's finished. I just have to nail the other two together—" When he saw her, he stopped. "What's wrong?"

She couldn't find the words.

He hurried to her side.

Tears pricked in her eyes and she realized saying the words would make what was happening real. But she had to deal with it. She couldn't pretend her life hadn't been turned upside down. "They want to take Jakie away from me and I don't know if there's anything I can do!"

Chapter Four

Nick pulled a kitchen chair close to Faith and sat facing her. "Tell me what happened," he said gently.

"The...caseworker found a couple to adopt Jakie."

"And?"

"And when she told me, I realized I don't want to give him up. I can't."

He heard her anguish. Seeing her and Jakie together, he realized how deep a bond they'd formed.

"Did you tell her that?"

She shook her head. "No. I was too stunned. I came into this thinking I'd care for Jakie until they found a family for him. It's been six months and we've been taking one day at a time. But I love him now, Nick. I can't let him go."

"Adopt him yourself."

Her brown eyes were wide, as if she'd never entertained the possibility. "I'm single."

"I don't think that matters anymore."

"It matters when the parent has a sporadic income

like I do. I can go several months without a contract. I plan for that, but I'm not sure how it will look on a home-study report. And the real problem is that there's a couple interested in Jakie now. How can I compete with them?''

Nick's heart started pounding. Suddenly in that instant, he saw something within his grasp that had always seemed out of reach. He fell silent...thinking, analyzing, wondering. Was he crazy to think Faith might even consider the idea that had flashed in his mind as if it was the most plausible solution to consider?

Clearing his throat, he began with the hypothetical. ''What if you were married? What if you had a stable income because your husband made a good salary and you still worked at home, able to give plenty of time to the child you want to adopt?''

''That's a terrific scenario, Nick, but...'' Her voice trailed off as she gazed at him with so many questions he couldn't possibly answer. Except for one.

''What if we married, Faith? Would that give you the leverage you need?''

''How could we marry, Nick? You don't even live in Winding Creek. You don't *want* to live in Winding Creek. You have a business in Rutland.''

''And I've been planning to open another store. Why not in Burlington? I'd have to travel back and forth every week or two, but it's workable.''

''Why? Why would you do this? Nick, do you even realize what you're suggesting?''

''I'm suggesting that we give a home to a little boy who's already lost too much.'' Nick knew about loss and what it did to a child inside, how it made him feel as if he wasn't worthy of anyone's love.

"But this is a commitment."

Nick pushed back his chair and stood. "You don't believe I can make a commitment?"

When she stood, too, her hands fluttered in the air. "I don't know! This whole idea is crazy."

He took her hands in his and brought them to his lips. "Is it? You tremble when I touch you. You arouse me. A little boy who loves you very much could be torn from you on the decision of a caseworker or if it goes further, a judge. We could make a life together, Faith."

She closed her eyes for a moment, then opened them again. "Why haven't you married again? Why ask me? You could have any woman you want..."

His gut clenched and he released her hands. "You make it sound so easy. It's not. Why haven't you married?"

Blushing, she turned away and walked to the other side of the room. "I've never fallen in love again."

"And who knows what love is, Faith? Attraction? Excitement that fades? The truth is—I haven't married again because I haven't found a woman I could trust and respect. I know trust has to grow. But I respect you, Faith. I always have. I think we could build something solid."

"Nick, this would be such a gamble. What if we get married and the agency decides the other couple would be better suited for Jakie. Then what?"

"Then we take it as it comes. We don't give up without a fight. We regroup when we have to and make decisions that are best for all of us."

Faith brushed her hair over her forehead and looked so troubled Nick wanted to put his arms around her. But he didn't want to tip the scales the wrong way.

After a long pause, she came back to the table. "We can't make this kind of decision overnight. We both need time to think..."

The front door opened and Jakie ran through the living room to the kitchen, golden wings flapping behind him. "See my wings? See my wings? Aren't they great? Grandma Hewitt says we can make more for the other kids."

As Constance followed Jakie into the kitchen, Nick realized Faith was right. They *did* need to think. He wouldn't just be marrying her, but her family. And even if they moved away...

Would Faith ever move away? Could he be happy in Winding Creek if she wouldn't?

Questions they needed to discuss along with hundreds of others. But one thing he was sure of. He didn't regret his proposal. The family he'd always dreamed of was almost in his grasp.

Nick had discovered something interesting about Faith since his proposal on Wednesday. Jitters drove her to clean. After they'd gone grocery shopping Wednesday evening, he had helped her put Jakie to bed. Afterward, she'd cleaned all the kitchen cupboards. He had offered to help, but she'd waved him away, the turmoil inside her evident with her quick movement of canned goods from one side of the shelf to the other. Yesterday, throughout Thanksgiving dinner with her parents, she'd pretended nothing was wrong. But every time he'd found her gaze on Jakie, he could see the anguish, her attempt to weigh the pros and cons of the best decision for the little boy she'd come to love.

This morning she'd cleaned out the refrigerator,

dropped a quart of orange juice and broken a glass. And he still didn't know what she was thinking. The more he was around her and Jakie, the more he longed for connections and the grounding he'd never had.

When a BMW drew up to the snow-piled curb out front, Nick saw the fear on Faith's face. "Have you made a decision?"

"Nick, you make this sound so easy. I've had forty-eight hours to think about something that will affect all of us for the rest of our lives!"

He heard the panic in Faith's voice and couldn't help taking the sponge from her hand. She'd used it to wipe down the counters. Determined, he held her by the shoulders so she couldn't evade him as she had the past two days. "Sometimes you have to act on instinct. Sometimes you just have to do what your gut tells you is right. Jakie shouldn't be separated from you and you know it."

"But to marry you..."

Backing away, he crossed his arms over his chest. "Is the thought so abhorrent? Because if it is..."

"No! I just..." She rubbed her hand across her forehead. "This isn't the way I ever imagined marriage. I'm still hoping the Brewers will meet Jakie and decide they want an infant or a little boy with blond hair instead of red."

"You're in denial. Any couple would love Jakie..."

The doorbell rang and Faith's complexion paled. "I'll get it."

It was obvious the Brewers were a well-to-do couple, from the car at the curb, to Mrs. Brewer's cashmere coat and designer suit, to Frank Brewer's fine leather jacket and shoes. Because Nick had grown up poor, he knew the cost of what he couldn't have.

During the next hour, Faith introduced Nick to Darla and the Brewers as a good friend. Then she told Jakie the couple had come especially to meet him. Nick watched the way the Brewers tried to coax the five-year-old to play with them, to build with blocks, to color. But Jakie must have sensed something was amiss. He answered the couple when they asked him questions, but he stayed close to Faith, following her direction. She was acting as intermediary, and Nick bet it was killing her. At one point, Frank Brewer took Darla Granger aside in the kitchen. A few minutes later they came back to the living room.

With a smile for all of them, Darla said, "Why don't we set up another meeting for next week. Maybe the Brewers could take Jakie for lunch..."

"No!" The word burst from Faith as if she'd been holding it inside for two days. "Darla, can I speak to you in private?"

Darla looked puzzled. "Certainly."

The Brewers exchanged a look and then Frank Brewer said, "We'll wait outside." In a flourish of coats, they said goodbye to Jakie, telling him they'd see him again soon, and went out on the front porch.

As soon as Faith closed the door, she said to Jakie, "Honey, would you go play in your room for a little while?"

"Can Nick come, too?" Jakie asked.

"Give me a few minutes, sport. Then I'll be up," Nick answered.

That seemed to satisfy Jakie because he took off up the steps.

Faith waited until they heard the sound of his feet in the hall upstairs before she turned to Darla. "I want to adopt Jakie."

Frowning, Darla said, "You knew this was only a temporary arrangement. I know this is hard..."

"It's not hard. It's impossible. Nick and I are getting married and we want to adopt Jakie."

"Married? Faith, I hope you're not doing this..."

Nick stepped beside Faith and circled her waist with his arm, felt her tense then relax. "Faith and I have known each other since high school. This situation with Jakie has made us realize how much we want a life together."

Darla shook her head. "Faith, I wish I had known this before. You should have told me about your marriage plans."

"To be honest, Miss Granger, we've decided to get married as soon as possible because of Jakie. We want him to feel secure," Nick said.

With a worried look, Darla glanced from Faith to Nick. "The Brewers are involved now, which makes this more complicated. Mr. Brewer told me they like Jakie. They want to set up regular visits."

"But we're going to adopt," Faith protested.

"Unfortunately it's not that simple. If you do marry now and apply for adoption, your home-study process will take much longer. We will have to be sure you have a stable marriage." Darla peered outside at the couple who had walked down the steps. "I'll talk to the Brewers and get back to you."

Nick opened the door for the caseworker. After she'd met the Brewers on the walk and gone to their car, he turned to Faith. She looked unsteady and he pulled her into his arms. "It will be all right," he murmured above her head.

Pushing back, she asked soberly, "Do you really

want this marriage? Are you ready to go through tons of questions and strangers probing into our lives?''

He thought about his background, how he'd been ashamed of it most of his life until he realized it didn't have to affect his future. "I'm ready. Faith, I never had a family. My mother bailed out when I was four. And Dad... When I was growing up, he wasn't really there. I know we can make a good home for Jakie. And I think we can make each other happy, too. Haven't you ever taken a risk?''

It was a few moments before she spoke. "No, I haven't. And maybe it's time. I can't lose Jakie. I'm ready to marry you, Nick, as soon as you'd like.''

Her skin was so soft, her eyes such a stunning brown, the golden sparkle there making him ache for her and the life he hoped to share with her. He stroked the delicate point of her chin, then her lower lip. Bringing his lips to hers, he took her slowly with great care. As her hands wrapped around his neck, he brought her closer, making her aware of his desire.

"Nick, are you coming up?'' Jakie called from the upstairs hallway.

Knowing the five-year-old had to come first, Nick broke the kiss and stepped away. "I'll be right up.'' He kissed Faith's forehead. "We'll talk after Jakie goes to bed.''

As he climbed the stairs, he realized he'd rather make love to Faith than talk, but he knew he couldn't push her. They had to go slowly to build the foundation they all needed.

At bedtime, Nick joined Faith in Jakie's room, feeling a new joy when he looked at the child, knowing it was more likely than not that he was actually going to be a father. He sat at the foot of the bed and listened as Faith read Jakie a story, watching her as much as the little boy.

After the story, Jakie looked up at Faith. "Why did those people come today?"

Faith glanced at Nick then answered, "They're looking for a little boy or girl to love."

"I wanna stay with you. I don't wanna live with anybody but you."

She hugged the little boy tightly. "I'm going to do everything I can to make sure you can stay with me." With a kiss on his cheek, she added, "You let me worry about the grown-up stuff. Okay?"

Nick knew children didn't miss a trick. Adults didn't give them enough credit, sometimes. But distraction never hurt. "Tonight while you're falling asleep, you think about going to get that Christmas tree tomorrow."

There was pause, then Jakie gave Nick a wide grin. "An' hot chocolate an' cookies at school an' a horse."

"A horse pulls the wagon on runners through the field," Faith explained. "Then after the tree cutting, the mothers serve hot chocolate and cookies at the school. The kids play games."

The ring of the phone broke the bedtime routine, and Faith's expression changed from one of anticipating a Christmas tradition with Jakie to one of worry. "I should get that."

Nick knew she was hoping it was Darla—hoping the Brewers had changed their minds. "Go ahead. I'll make sure Jakie's tucked in."

Faith gave him a grateful smile and kissed the little boy she so much wanted to mother.

Tenderness for Jakie burgeoned in Nick as he lifted

the covers to the five-year-old's chin, tapped him on the tip of the nose and said good-night.

As he stepped into the hallway, he saw Faith standing in her office, staring at the receiver.

"Faith?"

She motioned to the stairs. "Let's go downstairs and talk." Keeping her voice low, she added, "I don't want Jakie to hear."

In the living room, she spun around, her hands clenched. "That was Darla. The Brewers called her. They saw their lawyer! They say I don't have any legal claim to Jakie. They want an evaluation of us as prospective parents and themselves and a decision made on that basis."

"Why can't they find another child?" Nick asked, understanding Faith's frustration...and fear.

"Apparently they've gone through years of infertility procedures. They don't want to wait any longer for a child, so they thought they'd adopt an older child rather than an infant. They feel Jakie's perfect for them..."

"He'd be perfect for anyone!" Nick exploded. "But he loves you. Can't they see it would be in his best interests to stay with you...with us?"

"Darla feels I...we...would have the edge. But she also hinted that money's not an issue for the Brewers. And if they push this and take it to court, anything could happen."

"The judge will follow Darla's recommendation, won't he?"

"We can hope..."

Nick clasped her by the elbows. "No, we can more than hope. We'll get married as soon as we can set it up, and we'll make sure Darla's evaluation of us is everything it needs to be. If the Brewers won't back off and we have the edge, then we're going to use it."

Faith's shoulders straightened and determination replaced the fear in her brown eyes. "What do we do first?"

Nick gave her a smile he hoped would encourage her. "You make a cup of tea, I'll get a soda and we'll plan the wedding." Then he kissed her lightly...for now. They'd have plenty of time to explore their desire after they set plans in motion to safeguard Jakie.

"What's going on with you and Nick Clark?" Margie Matson asked Faith as she helped her place cookies on trays in the elementary school lobby the following afternoon.

Faith and Margie had been friends since grade school. They didn't see each other as much as Faith would like. Margie was tied up with her three children, and Faith spent most of her time working or volunteering at the community center if she wasn't spending it with Jakie.

She couldn't announce her wedding plans to Margie when she hadn't even told her parents. Lord knew what *they* were going to say. She hadn't slept much last night as she'd thought and analyzed and thought some more about the plans she and Nick had made.

They'd tell Jakie about the marriage tonight. They'd tell her parents tomorrow. Nick would check on the license on Monday and they'd marry by the end of the week. Before the home-study started. They'd send a signal to the Brewers that they were serious about adopting Jakie.

On the one hand, Faith felt as if she'd be marrying a stranger. On the other, she felt as if she'd known

Nick all her life. She knew his background, his determination to better himself, the gentleness she felt when she watched him with Jakie or whenever he touched her. The one thing she didn't know was why he and Pamela Ann had divorced. But as they got closer, she was sure he'd confide in her.

She'd never taken the idea of marriage lightly. She wasn't now. She sensed that Nick needed a family almost as much as Jakie. But whether she could meet Nick's needs and make him happy was still very much a concern. Would the sparks of desire between them and their concern for Jakie be enough to form a union that would last? Her experience with men was so limited. And Nick...

Truly not knowing how to answer Margie's question, she simply said, "Nick's staying with me."

Her friend's blond ponytail slipped over her shoulder as she rubbed the small of her back. "I might be pregnant, but I'm not blind. When he came back from the wagon ride with Jakie, I saw him put his arm around you. I saw his smile. I also know he's sticking around longer than he planned. So if you don't want to tell me, just say so and I'll butt out."

Not wanting to shut Margie out, because she intended to ask her to be her matron of honor after she told her parents she was getting married, Faith smiled. "Nick and I are getting closer."

Margie tilted her head and studied her. "And that's all you're going to say."

Faith nodded, her gaze on Nick as he helped Bud and another father set the Christmas tree in its stand while the children listened to their teacher read them a story nearby.

Tony Winthrop, a divorced father who Faith had met

on numerous occasions at the community center and school functions, approached them and took a cookie from the tray. "The kids really enjoyed themselves this afternoon. They get a kick out of riding in those old wagons with runners."

Faith laughed. "I think Jakie was more excited about being able to pet a horse than cutting down a Christmas tree."

"That fellow with Jakie. I've never seen him around before."

Margie made no attempt to hide the fact that she was listening when Faith said, "Nick and I went to school together."

"Great. It's good getting together with old friends over the holidays." Tony smiled. "And maybe some new ones. I know you've been busy the past few months with Jakie, but I was thinking maybe we could go out to dinner sometime. Get to know each other better."

For the past year since Tony and his son had moved to Winding Creek, he'd never shown any interest in her. Or if he had, she'd missed it. They'd spoken a few times, about school activities...about the pageant. Tony wasn't as tall as Nick, slimmer in build. He was handsome in a refined way, not with the strong lines that delineated Nick's features.

Nick.

Faith glanced over at him and his gaze was on her. He was frowning.

"Um, Tony, Nick and I are...seeing each other."

The man's face flushed. "Oh. I guess I waited too long to ask you out. But, hey..." He shrugged. "If things don't work out, who knows."

As Tony moved away, Margie nudged her arm. "So it's serious, isn't it? With Nick."

Faith suddenly realized her teenage crush had turned into something much deeper the past few days. She was falling in love with Nicholas Clark, and on her side, this marriage would be more than a marriage of convenience. That's probably why the idea scared her so. "Yes, it's serious."

Jakie was quiet on the way home, tired from the excitement and activities of the day. But Nick was quiet, too. Every once in a while he glanced at her, his blue eyes sparked with silver and she wondered what he was thinking. Maybe the day of being around families and more children had given him second thoughts.

At home, Faith helped Jakie with his jacket and boots and suggested he lie on his bed with his teddy for a short while before supper. When he didn't argue with her, she knew he was *really* tired.

Faith asked Nick, "Would you like a cup of coffee or something while I'm fixing dinner? I can put it on."

"If we're going to be married, Faith, you'll have to stop treating me like a guest." His voice was gruff, his jaw set.

"If? Are you having second thoughts?"

"No. But I wonder if you are."

"Why would you think that?"

"Tony Winthrop. The way he looked at you. Is there something going on?"

"You don't think I would have told you?"

Nick raked his hand through his hair. "Did you date him?"

"No. He asked me out today for the first time."

Nick's scowl was forbidding. "And you said..."

She felt unsure. "I said I was seeing you."

"Seeing me?"

His question made her feel defensive. "Well, what was I supposed to say? We haven't told anyone yet that we're getting married."

After studying her, he responded, "I know this is awkward for you and you're nervous about telling your parents."

"I didn't mean to snap," she said with a sigh, realizing he might be feeling as off balance as she was.

With a grin, he said, "That wasn't much of a snap. We've got to forget about always being polite, Faith. Honesty is the key here."

"It just seems so strange, thinking about being married in a few days."

"I hope you mean 'strange' in a good way."

"I'm just not always sure what to do or say."

He nodded. "I know. Like this afternoon. When that guy was putting the make on you, I wanted to come over, put my arm around you and tell him to get lost. I have to admit, I never felt jealous like that before."

Her heart beat faster. "You were jealous?"

He slipped his hand under her hair and drew her closer. "Very jealous." With a seriousness that deepened the blue of his eyes, he added, "I want a real marriage, Faith. Loyalty, fidelity, the knowledge we'll make important decisions together."

The conviction in his voice made Faith wonder if he hadn't experienced that kind of marriage with Pamela Ann. But the thought seemed to evaporate as his lips settled on her mouth and he brushed them back and forth across hers until she couldn't stand the teasing. She laced her fingers in his thick hair to tell him she wanted more. He didn't hurry. His tongue taunted her upper lip and she opened her mouth. But instead of dashing inside, he stroked her back, his hand coming to rest intimately on her buttocks.

Once again she was torn between wanting more and the knowledge that she and Nick had to build their relationship slowly or everything could come tumbling down.

He must have sensed her hesitancy because he pulled back and asked, "What's wrong?"

Her cheeks flamed but she knew she had to say what was on her mind. "You said you want this to be a real marriage. I do, too. But…I've only been with one man, Nick. A few times. I'm not sure what you expect from me. I can't just slip into bed with you without knowing more about you…about your life."

At first she thought he might be angry. But then he took her hand and pulled her to the sofa, tugging her down beside him. "If you're asking about my sexual history, I've always been careful. Except once. But that was years ago. I've been tested and the truth is—I haven't been with a woman for a long time. The risks of one-night stands are too great and I haven't looked for more. Until now."

"I'm not trying to pry."

"Don't apologize for asking questions that you have the right to know the answers to."

Did she have the right to know about his first marriage? "Tell me what happened with you and Pamela Ann."

When he looked away, she wondered if he was going to answer. But then he said, "We were too young to even think about marriage. It was a mistake from the outset."

"Did you want the divorce or did she?"

"I did."

His words hung in the air between them.

Nick shifted away from her and then stood. "I have to call and check in with my manager. Do you mind if I use your office?"

"No. Go ahead. I'll start dinner."

After he crossed the room, he paused at the bottom of the staircase. "When I'm finished, we can see if Jakie's awake and tell him we're getting married."

Faith just nodded, thinking about the divorce Nick had asked for. There was something he wasn't telling her. She was sure of it.

You can't learn everything about each other in one conversation.

She just had to remember Rome wasn't built in a day and their marriage couldn't be, either.

They'd have to lay the foundation one day at a time.

Chapter Five

"Where's Jakie?" Constance asked as she ushered Faith and Nick into the living room where Faith's father was watching a Sunday afternoon football game.

"He's playing with George at Bud and Margie's," Faith responded, her palms sweating.

Jakie had taken the news of her impending marriage to Nick with great enthusiasm. He'd asked Nick, "You'll be stayin' here with us?" When Nick said he would, Jakie had given him a hug and said, "I'm glad." It was as if the two had formed a bond from the moment Nick had rescued Jakie at the community center. But Faith doubted if her mother would understand that sudden bonding or her own connected feeling to Nick.

"Margie's due around Christmas, isn't she?" her mother asked.

"Yes." Small talk was difficult for Faith this afternoon with the announcement of her marriage on her mind.

Faith's mother sat in the recliner that matched her husband's. "Tom, can you turn that off so we can visit?"

Her dad smiled at her and Nick, and flicked off the television.

No sooner had Faith and Nick seated themselves on the sofa when her mother asked Nick, "So how much longer are you staying in Winding Creek?"

"That's what Faith and I have come to tell you. We're getting married."

It only took an instant for the words to sink in. In loud, stunned astonishment, her mother asked, "You're what?"

"Mom and Dad," Faith began calmly, though she was feeling anything but calm. "Nick and I will be getting married at the end of the week and we'd like you to be there."

The clock on the mantel ticked off second after second of silence as Constance and Tom Hewitt exchanged a parental look of concern.

"Faith, I want to talk to you in the kitchen," her mother demanded, standing and waiting for her daughter to do the same.

"That's not necessary, Mom. Anything you have to say, you can say in front of Nick."

"I don't think so, Faith Elizabeth. Please show me the courtesy of a few private moments."

Faith knew if she didn't deal with her mother now, she'd have to deal with her eventually. Nick must have sensed that because he leaned close to her and murmured, "Go ahead. Your dad and I will talk."

She gave Nick a grateful smile, realizing again what a strong and caring man he was. After she followed her mother to the kitchen, she asked, "Do you want me to make tea?"

"No," Constance returned. "I want some answers. What's going on? You can't marry Nicholas Clark. Not after a few days of seeing him again after all these years. Your father and I taught you to have more good sense than this. You don't only have yourself to think about but Jakie..." Her mother stopped abruptly. "That's it, isn't it? Jakie. What's happened?"

Faith knew the caseworker would probably talk to her mother and father during the course of the home-study so she had to be careful about what she said. "There's a couple who wants to adopt Jakie. *I* want to adopt Jakie." She hastily amended, "Nick and I want to adopt Jakie."

Constance sank into one of the oak plank chairs. "You can't adopt him yourself?"

"This couple...they've already seen a lawyer. Nick and I feel we have a stronger position if we're married. I can't give up Jakie, Mom. I love him and he loves me. He's already been through enough."

"Lord knows you're the child's anchor. Anyone can see that. But, Faith, marriage to a man you hardly know? Why is Nicholas willing to sacrifice himself?"

Her mother's words hurt. Couldn't she see marriage to Faith might be something Nick could look forward to? "Nick has never known a real family. He'd have one with me and Jakie."

"Oh, child. Men with backgrounds like Nicholas's don't know anything about family. They leave at the first sign of trouble. Even if he stays till the adoption goes through, what makes you think he'll stay after-ward?"

All the doubts that already plagued Faith came to

life in her mother's questions. "He says he knows the meaning of a promise."

"Knowing it and keeping it are two different things."

Faith knew her mother would try to argue with her till she saw her point of view. She wouldn't. Not this time. "I'm going to marry Nick. Nothing you say will change my mind."

Her mother studied her for almost a minute. "You're not just doing this for Jakie, are you? You have feelings for this man. Honey, I hope they're the right ones, not just some attraction..."

Faith took her mother's hand. "I'm marrying Nick and we'd like you to be there. Will you come?"

All the concern in Constance's eyes coalesced into support for her daughter. "If you get married, we'll be there. But, honey, please think about this more. Make sure you know that it's truly what you want to do and that you know the consequences."

The justice of the peace, Tobias Terry, lived on a farm on the west end of Winding Creek. The old farmhouse was huge, and Faith realized her marriage to Nick was all in a Friday evening's work for Tobias. He showed her parents, Jakie, Margie, Bud and Darla Granger to a wood-paneled room with a small podium and ten folding chairs. She and Nick had discussed inviting Darla and decided her witnessing this wedding could only solidify their position.

Tobias looked kindly at her and Nick, rubbing his gray beard. "Now don't you be nervous. Folks get married every day and live to tell about it." He smiled at his attempt at levity. "My wife and I have been married forty-one years, Faith, and been happier together than we could ever be apart. You've probably seen that with your own parents.''

He clapped Nick on the shoulder. "It's good to see you all grown up and ready to settle down. A smart man waits for the right woman, especially if he tried marriage when he was too young to make it work.''

Faith watched Nick's jaw tense and she could imagine what he was thinking. Everyone in Winding Creek knew everyone else's business.

He looked so handsome in his charcoal suit, dress shirt and tie that her heart couldn't keep a regular rhythm. Since the visit to her parents, they'd gotten caught up in preparations—the marriage license, buying wedding rings, Nick driving back to Rutland to talk to his store manager and pick up more than vacation clothes. He'd stayed overnight and returned late last evening.

And she'd thought about the consequences of marrying him. She could protect Jakie and hopefully keep him with her. The other consequence, that she might lose her heart, seemed secondary.

On the other hand, while Nick was gone, she couldn't get her mother's questions out of her mind.

Why is Nicholas willing to sacrifice himself? Even if he stays until the adoption goes through, what makes you think he'll stay afterward?

Faith didn't know the answers.

Did Nick feel as if he was sacrificing himself? When they'd said good-night last night, he hadn't kissed her. He hadn't kissed her since her questions about his first marriage. But this evening when she'd appeared downstairs, she'd thought she'd seen the sparks of desire in his eyes. Her white wool dress had a slightly flared skirt and softly fell to her knees. She'd swept up her hair, off her neck, curled it in the back, then attached a small wispy veil. With the gold earrings her parents had given her for graduation in her ears, she'd felt pretty and excited and hopeful. Now, as Nick offered her his arm to escort her to the front of the room, butterflies fluttered in her stomach at the intense look in his blue eyes. They were actually getting married.

Tobias Terry preceded them to the front. After a few steps, Faith stopped and had to say, "Last chance, Nick. Are you sure you want to do this?"

He covered her hand with his, his expression serious. Then he looked at Jakie. "I'm sure."

Faith walked with him toward the lectern, her heart pounding.

Nick glanced down at his bride-to-be and stopped with her before Tobias, facing forward.

As the justice of the peace welcomed everyone, Nick savored the feel of Faith's hand in his and thought about his trip to Rutland where he'd spent time in the store, making sure everything was running smoothly in his absence. He hadn't told his manager about the wedding, just that he was going to stay in Winding Creek a while longer and take his vacation there. He was concerned if he told Greg about his marriage, even looking into another store location, his manager and his other employees might be concerned about their jobs, the possibility he'd close the store in Rutland in favor of a bigger one in Burlington. Until he found a location and actually put a plan into action, it was better if Greg thought he was just taking a longer vacation.

Truth be told, he also hadn't wanted to go into an explanation to practical strangers about his sudden wedding. His personal life was no one's business but his.

Yesterday afternoon and evening had seemed to drag until the Toy Station closed. Afterward he'd gone upstairs to his apartment. It had been silent. Empty. An emptiness he hadn't truly realized until he'd accepted Faith's invitation to stay in her home.

Finished with preliminaries, Tobias Terry now called on Nick and Faith to say their vows. As Nick looked down at his soon-to-be wife, repeating promises, remembering the lie of his first marriage, he knew he was setting his life on a new course...with Faith and Jakie. In her white dress, her hair so delicately touchable, her lips the most inviting pale pink, he wondered how Faith thought of him—if she only saw him as a solution. Because he wanted more from this marriage than being a father to Jakie.

When the justice of the peace pronounced them husband and wife and said with an age-old smile, "You may kiss the bride," Nick took full advantage of the tradition.

Faith looked shy and very vulnerable. Gentleness overtook his need to possessively claim her. His lips settled on hers, his tongue slipped into her mouth and he stroked her with a quiet intensity that snatched his breath.

When he heard someone clear his throat, he pulled back, his arm still encircling his new wife. She was flushed and seemed highly embarrassed. He wondered how long it would take until she would become his wife in every sense of the word. Telling himself Faith was skittish because her parents were watching, he murmured to her, "When we're alone, we can take this as far as we'd like."

Before she could respond, Jakie hopped off his chair and ran to them. "Are we married now?"

"We're married now." He stooped and picked up Jakie, holding him in his arms, knowing he'd made the best decision of his life.

Back in her own kitchen a few hours later, Faith stared at the two white doves perched on the small top layer of their wedding cake. Her mother had hosted a small reception for them complete with the cake, and then given her and Nick the top layer to take home insisting that was the traditional thing to do.

Faith removed the doves from their latticed perch on the icing, then couldn't help but lick the white confection from her finger.

"Caught you," a deep masculine voice teased from the doorway.

Holding out the thumb she didn't lick, she impulsively offered, "Want some?"

Nick's blue eyes deepened as he crossed to her. He'd discarded his suit coat and opened the collar of his shirt. But he still wore his tie and he looked every bit as handsome as he had when he'd said, "I do."

Lightly, but with firm strength, he clasped her wrist. When he slowly brought her thumb to his mouth, her knees felt weak. His lips were dry but warm...so warm. His tongue touched her thumb and her breath caught.

He licked her thumb, then for an interminable moment he sucked the tip. Her insides trembled with a need that was exciting and new and scary. When he released her wrist, she stepped back, shaken by feelings that could hurt her deeply if this marriage of expediency didn't work.

Sacrifice himself.

With his background.

Faith didn't dismiss the doubts because they were

very real and could keep her safe...for a little while at least. "Jakie's sound asleep?" she asked, searching for a topic of conversation.

Nick's knowing look told her he knew she was trying to distance herself. "I looked in before I came down. He had a big day, too."

"Mom's buffet for us was nice. I told her not to go to a lot of trouble, but she did."

"You're their only child. You're lucky to have two parents who have always cared so much."

"I know I am."

"Your mother did an admirable job of being polite to me. We'll have to thank her because I'm sure Darla Granger took note."

"Nick, Mom will come around. She just thinks..."

"That we don't know what we're doing." He finished the sentence for her.

Faith wasn't about to express her mother's doubts about their marriage. Instead she said, "When you were talking to Bud and Margie after the wedding, Darla asked me if we were going on a honeymoon. I told her we were going to wait...that we wanted to give Jakie time to adjust to being a family."

"Good answer." Nick ran his finger along the icing on the edge of the cake. When his lips came around his finger, Faith remembered how they'd felt on hers.

"Do you want to go on a honeymoon?" he asked casually.

She felt her face getting hot. There was one purpose for a honeymoon and they both knew it. "I suppose we should just wait and see..."

Leaning against the counter as if he was very at home in her kitchen, he was quiet for a while, studying her. Finally he said, "We have to discuss sleeping arrangements. You can bet when Darla starts her home visits, she'll ask Jakie leading questions. We can't have him telling her we sleep in separate rooms.''

Faith needed something to do other than gaze into Nick's blue eyes and wonder about making love with him for the first time. Opening a drawer, she removed a box of plastic wrap. ''What do you suggest?'' She tore off a piece and set the cake on top of it.

Nick waited until she finished and remained silent until she looked at him. ''Do you trust me?''

Trust was complicated. She knew he was a good man…a strong man…and she felt safe in his presence. Trusting him to stay was another matter. ''I married you.''

''Then, how do you feel about sleeping in the same bed and trusting me to respect you? Nothing will happen that you don't want to happen.''

Sleeping with Nick. Temptation at its ultimate level. She was concerned about her own resistance level and making sure she protected her heart, yet she *did* trust that he wouldn't force her into anything she didn't want. ''I know I'm safe with you. And I have a queen-size bed so we'll have plenty of room.''

He looked relieved. ''Good. Now that that's settled, how about another piece of wedding cake?''

Smiling, she said, ''I'll put on the coffee.''

''Decaf. We wouldn't want to have trouble getting to sleep,'' he warned, a teasing note in his voice.

She turned toward the coffeepot, already thinking about lying in bed beside him.

The sound of the shower running distracted Nick as he prowled around Faith's bedroom. In his mind's eye, he could see her naked in that shower. He swore.

KAREN ROSE SMITH 85

He'd been the one who'd suggested this sleeping arrangement, and not only for the caseworker's sake. He'd thought if Faith got used to him being around in a more intimate way...

What, Clark? You wouldn't have to remain celibate?

Of course he didn't want to remain celibate. He was married!

Yet from Faith's shy responses, her blushes, her obvious uncertainty, he had to be patient.

He knew how to be patient. He'd been patient waiting for his mother to return since he was four. He'd been patient with teachers who'd thought he'd never amount to anything. He'd been patient with his dad, hoping someday they could have sober discussions like fathers and sons should. That patience had paid off.

He'd been patient with Pam until he'd learned she'd lied to him to get him to marry her. When he'd discovered she wasn't pregnant, had never been pregnant, he'd known their marriage was a sham and there was nothing left to salvage.

He'd married Pam because he'd thought he'd fathered a child. And now he'd married Faith because he wanted to be a father and a husband. There was no comparison. Faith didn't have a deceptive or manipulative bone in her body. They were beginning with honesty, attraction and a true affection he knew could grow.

If he was patient.

The water stopped running.

Nick sat on the edge of the bed, the side of the bed with the nightstand that didn't hold a bottle of perfumed lotion, or a gold barrette or the script for the pageant. He'd left open the bedroom door. When he heard light footsteps, he looked up and realized patience had better reign over self-control tonight.

Faith stood in the doorway in a pink satin nightgown and robe, her hair soft and flowing around her face, her skin creamy above the satin, her scent as sweet and fresh as a summer garden. She must have used soap the same scent as the lotion. He'd seen the bottle of pink shower gel in the shower. He'd opted for the regular bar in the soap dish.

Suddenly he wished he'd bought Faith flowers, lit a few candles and persuaded her they should celebrate alone. Yet, he didn't want to coerce her.

She crossed to her side of the bed and lifted the sheet and blanket, crawling underneath.

Nick propped against the two pillows at the headboard. "Aren't you going to take off your robe?"

Hopping out of bed, blushing furiously, she quickly untied her belt, shrugged out of the robe and laid it over the small bedroom chair. Her gown had flowing elbow-length sleeves and a high waist. But even under the gathers of fabric he could see the outline of her breasts and his body responded.

This time when she crawled under the sheet, he pulled it over him, too, smoothing it over the two of them. The space between them was obvious because it really wasn't very much space at all.

Faith looked as if she was ready to take flight at his slightest movement. All he wanted to do was get her to relax or she'd be sleeping on the couch by morning.

Slowly, so he didn't startle her, he shifted on the bed to face her. "Happy wedding day, Faith." Leaning toward her, he kissed her forehead, then backed away and settled on his pillow.

He stared up at the ceiling and heard the click of the

light switch. With the minimum rustle of covers, she settled on her pillow a good six inches away. If she wasn't careful, she'd fall off the bed! The scent of her taunted him. Knowing she was less than an arm's length away kept him aroused. But he reminded himself again that patience was everything.

With that thought playing like a mantra in his mind, he rolled on his side away from her and prayed for sleep to come quickly.

The warm, snugly feeling surrounding Faith was so pleasant, she didn't want to wake up. Heat and strength against her back, a muscled arm encircling her waist...

A muscled arm. Her eyes flew open and sleep was a dream she couldn't remember. Good Lord, Nick's body pressed against hers, and through the satin she was very aware of his masculinity.

How was she going to extricate herself without waking him? How...?

"We must have gotten cold in the middle of the night." His voice was sleep-husky, deep, and an erotic vibration close to her ear.

If she turned, their bodies would rub together even more intimately. "I'll have to get an extra blanket out tonight."

It was the first thing that came into her head, but as soon as she said it, she realized he could take it as an insult. And when he withdrew his arm and slid to his side of the bed, she knew he had. Scurrying to sit up, pulling the covers with her, she hastened to say, "Nick, I didn't mean that I don't want you to touch me. Waking up like that was such a surprise..."

"Believe it or not, it was to me, too. Maybe our subconscious knows something we don't. If that kind of thing makes you uncomfortable, we can stuff a few pillows in the middle.''

The ball was definitely in her court. She suddenly realized snuggling with Nick wasn't something she wanted to dissuade. ''I like cuddling,'' she said, watching her new husband closely.

''So that's what you call it,'' Nick said with a shake of his head and a faint smile. ''Some men might consider it foreplay.''

The intensity in Nick's eyes said that's exactly what he'd like to consider it as he leaned toward her and kissed her.

The kisses they'd shared the past few days had been exciting, starting easy and escalating slowly. This kiss didn't have a beginning. It was full-blown from the start—demanding…possessive…totally   intoxicating. Nick's hand caressed her shoulder while his tongue told her exactly what he'd like to do.

''Faith! Nick! Can I have…?'' Jakie burst into the room and stopped when he saw them jerk apart.

Faith realized some new rules were in order and maybe an explanation. ''Honey, come here.''

Jakie ran to her and jumped up onto the bed.

''Jakie, now that Nick's living with us and we're married and sleeping in the same room, we'd like it if you could knock before you come in.''

'''Cause you don't want me to see you kissin'?''

Nick chuckled. ''Not exactly. Married couples just like to be alone sometimes with the door closed. But that doesn't mean you can't get us if you need us, or if you want to tell us something. It's just called respecting someone's privacy. As you get older, you'll probably want to keep your door closed some of the time, too.''

Jakie didn't seem to understand all of it completely, but he shrugged. "Okay. Can I have that crispy cereal for breakfast?"

Faith laughed. "Sure, you can. Go brush your teeth, then we'll pick out some clothes to wear."

Jakie vaulted from the bed and ran to the bathroom.

Turning to Nick, Faith said, "You handled that really well."

"I've found like with everyone else, honesty's the best route—even with kids. Though I do wish Jakie's timing had been a little better—"

The doorbell rang.

"Are you expecting anyone?" Nick asked, glancing at the bedside clock.

"Not at nine on a Saturday morning." She slipped out of bed and grabbed her robe. "I'll see who it is."

Nick pulled a pair of jogging pants and T-shirt out of one of the drawers Faith had emptied for his use. "You help Jakie. I'll get it."

Instead of watching Nick get dressed as she was tempted to do, she went to the bathroom to supervise Jakie brushing his teeth. But a few minutes later, Nick called her name. When she went to the top of the stairs, he said, "It's Miss Granger. She wants to start the home-study."

For the past few days, in preparation for the wedding and the day itself, Faith had almost forgotten the reason she and Nick had married. Darla's arrival made her realize she could still lose Jakie. And if that happened, she might lose Nick, too.

An hour later, when Nick closed the door on Darla Granger, he breathed a sigh of relief. He wasn't at all sure how the interview had gone. There had been some tense moments—like when Darla had asked if they'd be staying in this house or moving…like when she'd asked if they expected Jakie to go to college…like when she'd asked if Faith got along with Nick's family.

Nick had quickly explained that his mother had left her family when he was four and that he and his father had never heard from her again. Faith had added that Nick's father had moved away from Winding Creek years ago and she was looking forward to talking to him when he called.

Jakie had eaten cereal while the adults talked. When Darla had asked to speak with Jakie alone, Faith and Nick had made a pot of coffee and sipped it while they waited, only catching a few words now and then.

The whole thing had been awkward and stress-provoking. But he'd thought that under the circumstances, they'd handled it well. Still, he was glad to see Darla Granger drive away. Before he could join Faith and Jakie in the living room, he heard someone on the porch. The mailman poked letters through the slot in the door. Nick picked them up, shuffling through them. The beginning of the month. Electric bill. Telephone bill. Gas bill.

When he walked into the living room, the sight of Jakie and Faith on the floor, building with blocks, stopped him. Faith got a certain look on her face whenever she was near Jakie—it was tender and caring and made Nick hurt deep inside and he didn't know why.

He lifted the envelopes in his hand. "Utility bills. I'll write out the checks when I sit down with store business in the next day or so."

"We haven't discussed finances," she said quietly.

Maybe she didn't want him taking over. "We can look over the bills tomorrow and decide what we want to do. I thought I'd go to the community center today and finish up the panels. What are your plans?''

"I have rehearsal with the children at one.''

"Do you want me to wait to work on the scenery?''

"No. We're just going over their lines. They're not ready for the stage yet.'' She capped Jakie's shoulder. "Why don't you go get your coloring book and crayons to take along?''

Jakie nodded, scrambled off the floor and ran upstairs.

When he was out of earshot, Faith asked, "How do you think our meeting went with Darla?''

It was obvious Faith was worried. When he looked at her, he realized the fear of losing Jakie was always present, never far from her thoughts. "I think we smoothed over the rough spots.''

"But what if the Brewers don't have any rough spots?''

"Faith, no couple is perfect. Everyone has skeletons in their closet. Darla Granger seems like a sensible woman. What matters is the way you love Jakie, the way he loves you and the caring we're going to give him now that we're married.''

"I hope you're right.'' Faith picked up the plastic blocks and dropped them into a canister.

Nick realized nothing he could say would reassure her. Only the Brewers backing off could do that. He could only hope that as time went on, they'd lose interest or come to see Jakie belonged with Faith...and with him.

Chapter Six

While Nick concentrated on attaching wheels to the base of the first panel unit on Saturday afternoon, he didn't hear Constance Hewitt's approach. She had been helping Faith go over lines with the kids. Instinctively he glanced over his shoulder and found his new wife, surrounded by children, looking as if she was exactly where she belonged. He couldn't help looking at her often...he couldn't help wanting her. And wanting her to want him.

"This was an ingenious idea, Nicholas. Faith said you worked construction jobs for a few years."

With Faith's mother, he felt like a teenager again, defending himself, trying to prove something. "Yes, I did. It makes me handy around the house," he added with a smile, attempting to make a connection with his mother-in-law.

But Constance's expression didn't change and Nick realized she'd come up on the stage to discuss more than his construction skills. He waited.

"Nicholas, I'm not sure quite how to say this..."

"Straight out would be the best, Mrs. Hewitt."

"All right, then. I know why Faith married you, although she couldn't put it into words in case Miss Granger questions me. Faith loves Jakie as she's never loved anyone in her life. Her world revolves around him. Since she is the way she is, I think she'd given up the hope of ever marrying and having children of her own."

"I don't understand. What do you mean because Faith is the way she is?"

"Certainly you can see that she's always been backward and shy in social situations. Between men and women."

He wanted to ask whose fault that was—though he didn't think Constance's assessment was accurate. Faith might be quiet, but she certainly knew how to relate to anyone around her, and he sensed a passion simmering below the surface, in her kisses and responses, that he longed to explore. If Faith lacked self-confidence with men, and he hadn't seen the lack in any other areas of her life, he had a feeling the root of it lay with her mother.

But he didn't want to start a war. "Faith is a beautiful woman. She's caring and warm—"

"And easily taken advantage of. I don't want you taking advantage of her."

"I wouldn't do that."

Constance ignored him and plowed ahead. "She's a small-town girl. She might think she owes you whatever you ask for so she can keep Jakie."

Now he got it. Anger simmered at Constance's implication that he would demand sex in return for marriage, that he didn't respect Faith enough to consider what she wanted. "We *are* married, Mrs. Hewitt. And whatever happens between us is our business, not yours." He didn't want a war, but he did want boundaries.

"If this *marriage* doesn't work, it will be *my* business because I'll have to pick up the pieces when Faith gets hurt," Constance claimed.

Nick stood and towered over Faith's mother. "It's a shame you don't have the same high regard for your daughter that I do. Faith is a strong woman. It's an inner strength that isn't loud or self-proclaiming. She's always had it. Even in high school. I watched her debate and win. I saw her achieve even when it set her apart from her peer group. And I see it each day with Jakie, her wisdom in caring for him. Faith isn't the type of woman who falls to pieces. She'd find another goal and she'd move on."

"I won't see her compromised, Nicholas. If you're smart, you'll give her the space to grow into this marriage, until you both find out if marriage is really what you want."

Before Nick said something he'd regret, he reminded himself Constance was a mother protecting her daughter. But if he didn't walk away from her now, he might put an impenetrable wall between them. "I'll keep what you said in mind, Mrs. Hewitt. Now, if you'll excuse me, I need to go to the hardware store."

After being as polite as he could manage, he left the stage. Cold air was exactly what he needed. He plucked his jacket off the metal rack and went outside. When the community center door banged behind him, he thought about Faith, and space, and a marriage that wasn't yet real.

Two hours later, as parents filed into the community

center at the end of practice to pick up their children, Faith looked around for Nick. She'd seen him leave soon after they'd arrived. Aware of his return a short time later, she'd noticed him as he'd taken a few small boxes up on the stage. Now her gaze scanned the large room and found him by the kitchen talking with Bud.

Nick looked over at her, and instead of the smile she expected, he frowned and came toward her. When he faced her, there was something different in his eyes...a guardedness that hadn't been there before.

"Are you ready to leave?" she asked, wondering if he'd grown impatient when her practice session had run late.

"Not yet. I want to finish these so you can start painting. Matter of fact, I won't be back for supper. Bud and I are going down to Logan's Pub, watch ESPN and catch up."

This was the day after their wedding. They were newlyweds. She'd thought maybe they'd have a glass of wine after Jakie went to bed...talk...

"Would you rather I did it another time?" His expression gave no clue as to what he was thinking.

She couldn't put chains around him or make demands. That would make him regret this marriage even before it got started. "No. That's fine. There's a movie on television tonight I want to see." What a lame comeback! The picture of her in sweats in front of the TV would really make him want to rush right home.

"I'll tell Jakie I'll look in on him when I get home."

"I'm sure he'd like that." She felt so formal...so polite...as if they were housemates instead of husband and wife.

He nodded to the stage. "I'm going to get back to work. Don't wait up. I might be late."

After she gave him a smile that told him whenever he got home would be fine, he walked away.

Was her mother right?

Did Nick's background dictate that he'd eventually walk away from their marriage, too?

Music blared from the jukebox in Logan's Pub as two sportscasters on the television above the bar discussed highlights of the day's football games. Nick kept his eyes on the TV screen, but his thoughts were far from football as he and Bud sat on the high stools, popping peanuts into their mouths.

They'd eaten earlier at one of the barrel-like tables, rehashing old football plays and their high school escapades. Bud had steered clear of Nick's marriage to Pam. Now, sitting in the dimmer side of the bar, they'd fallen into an easy silence as Nick sipped on a soda and Bud lingered over a beer.

The song finished on the jukebox and none took its place. When the sportscaster went to commercial, Bud took a long swig of beer, then leaned against the short back of the stool. "So, are you going to tell me why you're sitting here with me tonight instead of taking advantage of being married?"

Taking advantage of being married. Taking advantage of Faith. Her mother's words, though Bud was using them differently. "There's nothing to tell."

"Remember me, ol' buddy? I'm the one who knew you talked and flirted more than you scored. I'm the one who knew you worked your tail off *after* football practice to make money so you and your dad could eat. I'm the one who knows you didn't touch liquor even back then because you didn't want to end up like your dad. There's something to tell here. Margie knows it, too.''

Nick knew Faith and Margie had been friends for years. But with Jakie's welfare at stake…

"I know what you're thinking," Bud went on. "Faith hasn't said anything to Margie. But let's face facts. Me and Margie were always like peanut butter and jelly. Everybody knew we'd get married. You and Faith… You were like night and day."

"She's different from other women I've known," Nick said. "She's honest clear through. We're going to build our marriage on honesty. No illusions. No make-believe."

"You're doing this because of the boy, aren't you? Rumor has it this caseworker brought a couple to meet him. And then no time later, the two of you get married."

"I can't talk about it, Bud."

"Um. Okay. I get the message. But I still think it's a bad idea for you to be here with me instead of at home with your new wife."

Another song played on the jukebox as Nick lifted his soda. Bud simply didn't understand. He had to give Faith some space. He had to let her get used to the idea of them being married. He had to give her time to know him.

Then maybe she wouldn't feel as if he was taking advantage of her when they made love.

It was an hour later when Nick let himself into the house. The porch light was burning. He usually forgot to turn on his at his apartment. Faith had given him a key, and as he let himself into the house, the feeling was altogether different than coming home to an empty apartment. Jakie and Faith were probably asleep, but the knowledge they were there filled his heart with a warmth that was new and comforting.

After making sure the house was secure downstairs, Nick climbed the steps and headed for Jakie's room. Because of a night-light glowing in the hall, he didn't have to turn on the overhead light. The five-year-old was sleeping on his side with his teddy bear tucked into his arm. But he'd thrown off his covers. The old house was drafty from the low temperatures and wind blowing outside. Nick pulled the sheet and blanket over Jakie's shoulder.

Would this little boy truly be his son someday? Could he and Faith form a bond that would last?

Faith. His wife. Patience.

It was better if he didn't wake her.

Thinking about slipping into the bed beside her made him realize it would be a hell of a lot easier if he slept on the floor!

He undressed in the bathroom where he'd left his sleeping shorts hanging on a hook on the door. When he entered the bedroom, he closed the door and used instinct to guide him to the bed.

He'd just slid under the covers when Faith's voice came through the darkness. "Did you have a nice evening?"

Nick sighed. So much for not waking her. "Bud makes it easy. He does all the talking."

Silence danced between them. Nick wanted to take Faith in his arms and kiss her. But with her sweet scent wafting around him, her satin gown sliding against the sheet, he knew kissing wouldn't be enough. Even if she consented to have sex with him, he wouldn't be sure if she felt coerced, or obliged. He didn't want her to make love to him out of a sense of duty or misplaced gratitude.

"Would you like to go to church with us tomorrow morning?" she asked into the darkness.

Church. How long had it been since he'd seen the inside of a church? "Do you want me to go along?"

"Nick, if you don't want to…"

"I think it's important we do things together with Jakie. In the afternoon, I need to drive into Burlington and buy a printer so I can set up my computer and get some work done, but church in the morning will be fine."

"If you want to use my computer and printer, feel free."

"I have everything I need on my laptop. If I buy a printer of my own, we won't get in each other's way."

There was a slight pause, then she said, "I'll probably go to Mom's and help her with costumes. You'll have peace and quiet to work."

When the night enveloped them again, Nick longed to reach across the bed. But instead, he said, "Good night, Faith."

"Good night, Nick."

He felt the rustle of the covers as she turned away from him. Then he rolled to his side, his back facing hers. He'd be patient if it killed him.

One bathroom. Two adults and a child getting ready for church. Faith took clothes for Jakie from his closet while she waited for Nick to finish in the bathroom. The past few mornings, he'd been up before her, dressed and gone downstairs before she needed to use the bathroom. But this morning, the alarm she'd set had awakened them both.

She wondered if he'd gotten more sleep than she had. Not intending to wait up for him last night, nevertheless she'd found sleep impossible. And after he'd returned... She'd been aware of every movement he'd made.

As she laid Jakie's good clothes on his bed, she said, "You start getting dressed. I'll be back in a few minutes."

She'd showered last night. Since Nick was still in the bathroom, she'd dress first, then fix her hair and makeup when he'd finished. In a hurry, she shrugged out of the satin robe and tossed it over the chair on her side of the bed. Then she gathered her nightgown and lifted it over her head.

The door opened while her arms were still raised in the air.

She felt the rush of cooler air from the hall, she heard Nick's startled intake of breath, and she realized nothing she could say or do could help her embarrassment or Nick's at the moment. With as much dignity as she could muster, she laid the nightgown on the bed.

Nick didn't back out of the room. He didn't move or attempt to say something polite. But his gaze burned her as it moved over her, and she stood silent.

Then just as abruptly as he'd entered the room, he turned away. "I should have knocked. I'll get my clothes and dress in the bathroom."

Grabbing her robe, she slipped it on, excited by the sight of his bare chest and hair roughened legs, the evidence of his masculinity under the sleeping shorts, the raspiness in his voice. She walked up behind him and touched his arm. "This is your bedroom, too. You don't have to knock. I'll just be...more careful next time."

Nick's blue eyes showed no emotion as he looked at her...none of his thoughts. "Right. We'll both be more careful." Pulling away from her, he went to the closet and removed a shirt and trousers, then he left the room.

She'd said the wrong thing. But she hadn't been sure *what* to say. Her heart told her she and Nick were pulling farther apart instead of coming together. Hopefully all they needed was time. As time passed, they'd find their way to each other.

They had to.

The cursor of his computer blinked at Nick later that afternoon as he sat at the kitchen table. He punched in a few numbers, then swore when he realized he'd repeated the figures he'd entered a few minutes ago. If only he could concentrate.

Yeah, like he'd concentrated in church. The minister had spoken about two minutes when Nick's mind had wandered into forbidden territory. The sight of Faith naked had riled his hormones, made him edgy, and increased the tension between them. He'd felt like a voyeur, unable to turn away. From her flushed cheeks and her shocked and vulnerable expression, he'd known she wasn't ready for more than a housemate.

If he could just get the picture of her out of his head...

The front door opened, and a few seconds later Jakie stood beside Nick, staring at the computer. "Wow! Is it as good as Faith's? She lets me play games. And I push these buttons..."

Before Nick could protest or move, his afternoon's work was wiped away.

"Jakie, you don't touch my computer. It's not a toy.

You just lost everything I did this afternoon!'' The strength of his voice had increased with each breath until his last word was almost a bellow.

Jakie's blue eyes grew huge and his chin quivered. As tears glistened, he ran from Nick through the living room and pounded up the stairs.

"How could you speak to him like that?" Faith accused from where she stood at the doorway to the kitchen. Before he could answer, she turned to go after Jakie.

But he moved faster than she did and he caught her arm at the foot of the stairs. "Let me go. I need to talk to him. Alone."

"I don't know, Nick…"

He could see the doubts in her eyes…the fear that he might make Jakie feel worse. "I know I messed up. But if I'm going to be Jakie's parent, *I* have to fix it." When she glanced up the steps, when he thought about last night and the space between them in the bed, he knew he had to push her. "If we're going to make this work, Faith, you have to learn to trust me."

She studied him so carefully, he wondered what she was looking for. But after a few moments, she responded, "All right."

Nick climbed the steps, not sure what he was going to say or do. When he saw Jakie curled up on his bed, hugging his teddy with tear streaks on his cheeks, Nick's heart almost broke. He had done this. More than anyone, he should know how harsh words damaged. His father wasn't a mean man. But as he drank, he'd become gruff, impatient and sometimes nasty. There was no excuse for trampling a child's feelings. None.

Pushing Jakie's door open, Nick asked, "Can I come in?"

Jakie didn't lift his chin from his teddy bear's head.

Entirely out of his element, he operated on instinct. "I'm sorry I yelled. I shouldn't have. You didn't know you weren't supposed to touch my computer."

Jakie still kept his arms tightly around his bear but he lifted his head. "Where's Faith?"

"She's downstairs. I told her I'd like to talk to you for a few minutes. Okay?"

"I guess you can come in," Jakie murmured.

As Nick sat on the bed next to the five-year-old, he said, "I have to learn how to take care of you."

His honest statement brought Jakie's gaze to his. "You don't know how?"

"Nope. Not like Faith."

"Why not?"

Not sure how much to tell a child, Nick's intuition told him the truth was best. "Faith grew up with a mom and dad who loved her very much. My mom left when I was younger than you. My dad wasn't around much."

It was obvious from the expression on Jakie's face that he was making the connection between them. "Did you miss your mom?"

"All the time." Nick slid closer to the small boy and put his arm around Jakie's shoulders. "I might need your help to learn how to take care of you."

"Faith can show you."

Nick had to smile. "I'm sure she can. But I need you to be patient with me and always remember I don't want to do or say anything that will make you feel bad. But I might make mistakes."

"Like pushin' the buttons on your computer."

"Yep."

Jakie looked up at him. "I'm sorry I messed up your work."

Nick shrugged. "It's okay. You didn't know that would happen. But the next time, ask me before you press something."

After a few moments of silence, Jakie said, "I like you livin' here."

Nick gave his shoulders a squeeze. "Good. How would you like to go outside and throw a few snowballs?"

"It's gettin' dark!"

"We'll turn on the back porch light."

"Okay! I'll get my coat."

As Jakie scurried from the bed, Nick saw the flash of jeans outside the door. Apparently Faith had been listening to their conversation. He was torn between the disappointment that she hadn't trusted him to handle Jakie gently and the understanding that she had to protect this little boy she wanted as her son. Without her trust, they wouldn't have a marriage. Maybe if they made love...

Time, Clark. Give her time. This had happened so fast they were all off balance. But if he had anything to say about it, they'd find their footing. And soon.

A light snow fell as Faith gazed out the kitchen window at Jakie and Nick. They were rolling a second ball of snow for the snowman they were building in the glow of the porch light.

After she'd listened to their conversation, she'd hurried to her office. It wasn't that she didn't trust Nick to deal with the situation with Jakie, but she felt so protective of the little boy that she wanted to make sure he didn't get more upset. She'd also wanted to listen in and learn about her new husband in the process.

Her new husband.

Ever since yesterday, he was keeping his distance and she didn't understand why. Yet, if she looked at the situation from his perspective, his behavior made good sense. Why would he want to kiss her and touch her if that's as far as she'd go?

Her upbringing and past experience with men led her to want to be sure of her feelings for Nick and his for her before she made love with him. Their physical attraction simply wasn't enough. Yet she couldn't expect Nick to stay in a marriage that wasn't a marriage.

Realizing that supper was cooking just fine on its own, she went to the closet for her coat and boots. When she stepped out on the back porch, Nick looked surprised.

"I thought you might need some help to finish before supper."

He nodded to the ball of snow he and Jakie had rolled. "We need a smaller one for the head."

Pulling her knit cap down over her ears, she clomped through the ice-crusted old snow and found a spot where she started packing. After Nick set the second large ball on top of the first, he sent Jakie inside for a carrot. Faith told him where he could find old buttons for the snowman's eyes and mouth. As she stooped over again to continue rolling the snowman's head, she was aware of Nick's gaze on her, of his profile—tall, strong and handsome—against the yellow porch light.

He moved toward her and her heart beat faster. Soon, his gloved hands were helping hers. The evening silence and the snowflakes falling softly seemed to emphasize the tension between them.

She straightened and stepped away as Nick mounted the smaller ball of snow on top of the others. Faith knew she had to break the silence. "It looks as if you and Jakie are friends again."

Nick packed the snow so the snowman's head was secure. "I apologized...asked him to be patient with me. He told me he was sorry for messing up my work. But then you know that, don't you? Because you were listening."

Even with the cold air whispering against her cheeks, they grew hot. "I wanted to make sure you wouldn't...that Jakie wouldn't get more upset."

She couldn't gauge Nick's expression as he turned from the snowman and concentrated on her. "Did I pass the test?"

An edge of anger definitely laced his words. "I never meant for it to be a test."

"But it was." His breath puffed out white into the cold air.

When she spoke, her breath visibly mingled with his. "You handled Jakie very well."

Laying his hands on her shoulders, Nick said, "I know what the stakes are. I won't do anything to hurt him."

She wished she could feel his hands, but between his gloves and her coat, she could only feel a slight pressure. "I know you won't." After seeing him with Jakie today, hearing them talk, she was sure of it.

Nick must have heard the certainty. The tense lines around his eyes lessened, and the look in them gentled. He kept studying her face as if he was searching for something. She wanted him to kiss her again. Why couldn't she be forward? Why couldn't she just reach out...

When Nick nudged her toward him, she didn't have to reach far. First she felt the cold still between them. But then his cheek brushed hers. His slight beard stubble was erotic, the tease of his skin exciting. She could feel the temptation of his heat, she could smell the scent of spice, she could hear the sound of his quickened breaths. The anticipation was almost as much torment as lying in the same bed with him last night and not touching.

He leaned back for a moment, and she couldn't help her sound of protest. His blue eyes probed her as he seemed to wait for something...for her to back away. She didn't want to back away and somehow she had to let him know. Leaning forward slightly, she hoped he'd read her signal.

Desire darkened his eyes and, as his lips sealed to hers, she was thankful he'd gotten her message. His strong arms encircled her and she pressed into him, wanting him to deepen the kiss. Lifting her arms around his neck, she worked off a glove and let it drop to the ground.

Too many clothes, too many barriers, too much distance. She tentatively touched his nape. It was hot with the body warmth she wanted to feel. She let her fingers play there until Nick's tongue slipped between her lips.

The heat of their desire seemed magnified by the cold. When his tongue stroked hers, she laced her fingers in his thick hair, relishing the feel of it, the sensation of being held in his arms. She trembled from the excitement, from the sheer pleasure, and as his hands stroked down the back of her coat, she wished they were inside...upstairs...with the door closed.

Their first kisses had been tentative explorations, man meeting woman curiously to discover if any pas-

sion was there. This kiss knew the passion was there
and built on it. With every sweep of Nick's tongue, he
took her deeper into it. It was the blaze of fire on a
snowy night, it was the beauty of snow and the danger
of ice, it was the promise of Christmas and her heart's
desire.

She'd never expected so much, yet she still wanted
more.

Bolder than she ever imagined she could be, she hes-
itantly touched his tongue with hers. His momentary
pause made her think he was going to pull away until
his arms closed her tighter against him. She tried it
again, and this time when their tongues met, she felt
his shudder. Could she arouse him the same way he
aroused her? Could her touch excite him, give him
chills, make him need her the way she was coming to
need him?

The kiss became a powerful connection, a source of
energy, a means of communicating desire that seemed
taboo otherwise. It seemed to go on and on and
on...leading one place...to a true honeymoon night.

Until abruptly Nick tore away.

If he hadn't been holding her, she might have fallen.
As she gazed up at him, the desire left his eyes and his
voice was controlled as he said, "I think maybe I
should sleep on the floor tonight."

Chapter Seven

As a snowflake fell on Faith's nose, she was truly embarrassed. But she knew she had to find out what had caused Nick's suggestion. "Why?"

"Because if you kiss me like that again anywhere near your bed, we're going to do more than sleep in it. Is that what you want?"

Her heart pounded hard and she knew all she had to do was say "yes" and they'd share a night she'd only dreamed of. But she wanted to share more than one night with Nick; she wanted to share a life. If they rushed into physical intimacy too fast without the feelings that should go with it, she knew she'd get hurt. Her attraction to Nick went far beyond the physical.

"I'm not sure either of us is ready for that."

"Oh, I'm ready," he said with a wry smile.

Her cheeks burned, even with the cold whispering over them. He ran his finger over her cheekbone in a tender gesture that urged her to fall into his arms again.

But she knew if she did, she had to be prepared for what happened next.

"I don't want to pressure you, Faith." His smile was gone; his tone was serious. "We both might sleep better if I bunk on the floor."

"If we move the futon in, Jakie might tell Darla."

With a shake of his head, Nick said, "We can't take that chance."

"I don't want you to have to sleep on the floor."

Raking his hand through his hair, he suggested, "Let's think about it. Tonight, I'll probably work late on the computer, and you'll probably be asleep when I come up. We'll see how that works."

She remembered last night and *not* being asleep.

Jakie slammed the back door and ran toward them, one of his gloves dangling in his hand, a carrot in the other. "I put the buttons in my glove," he said, lifting it to show them.

Nick patted Jakie's shoulder. "That was very clever. Let's see what you found."

As Faith watched Nick and Jakie form eyes and a mouth with the buttons on the snowman, her heart almost hurt from the joy of watching man and boy bond. In no time at all, Nick had added tree branches to the snowman's body for arms, and Jakie giggled at the way their snowman looked.

A few minutes later, they all went inside. After Faith helped Jakie remove his outerwear, he went to the living room to play.

Nick sniffed appreciatively. "Something smells great."

"I hope you like it. I just dumped the potatoes and carrots in with the chicken."

He hung Jakie's jacket over the counter stool so it

would dry. "I'm used to omelets, frozen food and take-out. Your meals get five stars from me."

The urge was so strong to ask him more about his marriage to Pamela Ann. Had she cooked for him? Had she kissed him back? Had she pleased him in bed? All questions that seemed much too invasive at the moment. So instead she asked, "Would you like to be Santa Claus for the community center's Christmas party? It's next Sunday."

"You don't have someone who usually does it?"

"Herb Dennison played Santa last year but he broke his hip and is still recovering. No one else has volunteered, so the job's open."

Nick grinned. "You know, I never even played Santa in my own store."

"What's the name of your store?" She'd never asked.

"The Toy Station."

"I like that. If you open a second store, would you call it the same thing?"

"Yes. It works. Sometime this week, I'd like to scout out sites in Burlington, maybe contact a real estate agent to see what's available."

Making plans like this filled Faith with hope that they could build a good life together...a strong marriage. "So you'd like to play Santa?"

"I'd like to *be* Santa. At least for one day. I can't imagine any job more rewarding."

With each day, with each conversation, she felt more for Nicholas Clark. She just wished she knew exactly what he felt for her.

The sun shone brightly, melting some of the four inches of snow that had fallen through the night, and

forming icicles on the eaves of buildings Faith passed
on Main Street on Monday afternoon. At the corner of
Main and Linden, she pulled open the door to the phar-
macy and stepped inside. She'd decided to pick up new
lipstick and nail polish on her way to the community
center.

Last evening she and Nick had sat down with her
finances. She was solvent with a small amount saved
for emergencies. He'd insisted on paying the utility
bills. She'd insisted on paying the mortgage. After they
put Jakie to bed, Nick had told her he didn't want her
to think twice about buying whatever she needed for
herself or Jakie, and he would open a checking account
for her to use for Christmas presents and anything else
she needed. He was being so generous.

Just like this afternoon. He'd told her he had to wait
for faxes and calls, but if she wanted to work on the
scenery, he'd watch Jakie. After his calls came in, he'd
bring Jakie and meet her at the center.

If only...

If only what? If only she'd *not* pretended to be
asleep when Nick came to bed at three a.m.? If only
she could forget the values that had been instilled in
her as a young girl? If only Nick could say he felt more
than desire?

She'd always been a dreamer. Maybe she should just
settle for respect and the chance to form a family and
keep Jakie.

Faith headed for the polish display and chose a deep
rose color and a matching lipstick. She was wondering
whether she should also buy blusher and eye shadow
when another display caught her eye.

Condoms.

She and Nick hadn't discussed having more children.

Of course, why would they when they hadn't even made love yet?

As she read one of the boxes, she heard Mrs. Barley, her mother's favorite gossip, in the next aisle. Faith could only see the top of her head but she could hear her clearly.

"Did you know Nicholas Clark married Faith? Can you imagine? No one even knew they were seeing each other. Constance is very closemouthed about it. I don't think she approves."

Faith started to move away. She didn't intend to listen to Winding Creek's version of her life. But as she picked up the box of condoms, she heard the woman with Mrs. Barley say, "That boy liked excitement. It's why he left. He sure won't get any with Faith—she's such a quiet little thing. Doesn't go out much. It won't last any longer than his first marriage. And it's no wonder. He had no proper example growing up."

The box slipped in Faith's hand and she almost dropped it. Just when she was starting to put her doubts aside, someone resurrected them like a small voice in her head that told her marrying Nick had been an impulsive decision that could have disastrous results. And if anything did happen between her and Nick, *when* it happened, she'd need the box in her hand. She would never trap him in a marriage he didn't want or put herself in a position to need something from him he couldn't give.

Becoming pregnant was definitely not a good idea.

The last fax whirred from the machine in Faith's office. He'd study the figures tonight then call Greg tomorrow about ordering additional inventory. Glad the last fax had finally arrived, Nick was about to call to

Jakie who was playing in his room when the phone rang. He picked it up and slipped the page with figures into a manila folder on Faith's desk. "Hello."

"Nicholas, it's Constance Hewitt."

"Faith is at the community center, Mrs. Hewitt."

"Actually...I, uh, have a problem. Our back porch roof collapsed."

"Were you or Mr. Hewitt injured?"

"Oh, no. Thank goodness. Tom went into Burlington for the afternoon. But I tried to call two contractors we know and we're not the only ones with this problem. They can't help us for a few days and we can't use our back door. Since you were once involved in construction, I was hoping you could do something."

"First I'll have to assess the damage and make sure it's only the roof that's the problem. Don't go near it, all right?"

"All right. Nicholas I know this is an imposition—"

"It's Nick, Mrs. Hewitt. And I'll be there in fifteen minutes."

An hour later, Nick had examined the damage and was removing the debris from the back of the house to the side. The flat roof on the small porch had held too many snows. He needed to go buy a few supplies so the cold and snow didn't get into the holes where the roof had torn away from the house.

He'd tried to reach Faith before he left and after he'd arrived here, but the line at the community center had been busy. Constance had told him she'd keep trying. He'd lugged a porch post to the pile of wood and shingles when he saw Faith coming around the side walk. He walked toward her, realizing he'd missed her in the few hours they'd been apart.

"Is there anything I can do?" she asked. "Mom called and told me what happened."

"I've got it covered. I'd like to get those holes patched up before dark."

"Mom can't reach Dad. He and a friend went to a decoy show. But he should be back soon. She's really grateful you could help."

"I don't want her gratitude, Faith."

"She's going to offer to pay you."

Nick shook his head. "I won't take it."

"I guessed that. But you know my mother will argue with you about it."

Standing near enough to Faith that their white breath comingled in the late-afternoon air, he didn't notice the cold...not when he stood this close to her. Suddenly he realized how important it was for Faith's parents to accept him. But even more important was his relationship with Faith. They needed some time alone together...time to concentrate on each other.

"Do you think your mom will be so grateful she'd do me a favor?"

Faith smiled. "If you won't take money, she'll trade. What kind of favor do you have in mind?"

"I'd like her to baby-sit Friday night. I want to take you dining and dancing...have some fun. What do you think?"

"I'd like that. A lot."

The soft look in Faith's eyes, the pretty curve of her lips, the way her hair softly brushed her cheek as the breeze caressed it, led Nick to believe an evening alone together could be more than a night out...it could be the real beginning of their marriage.

Looking into the dresser mirror Friday evening, Faith almost didn't recognize herself. She'd bought the dress that morning at the one small dress shop in Winding Creek while Jakie was at kindergarten. Nick had gone to her parents to make sure the patching he'd done on the back of the house was holding. After he'd cleaned up the porch debris in her parents' backyard and patched the house, they'd insisted he'd done enough and a contractor would take over the rest. Faith could tell her father liked Nick…a lot. And her mother…well, she'd warmed a little until her husband had suggested they keep Jakie overnight since it would probably be late when Faith and Nick came home from their night out.

Faith knew what her mother thought—that she was going to get hurt. But maybe it was time to take another risk.

She'd certainly done that when she purchased this dress! It was blue, silky and molded to her. The slit up the side was definitely daring. But she felt daring tonight. That's why she'd swept her hair up on top of her head, applied makeup, and added dangling pearl earrings to her ears. Finally she slipped on black high heels and headed for downstairs.

As she descended the steps, she saw Nick waiting for her on the sofa. He stood when he saw her and the darkening of his blue eyes encouraged her. She took her camel wool coat from inside the closet. But before she could slip into it, Nick was there, holding it for her. She slipped first one arm into it and then the other. His fingers brushed her neck as he adjusted her collar.

"Are you ready?" he asked, his voice husky.

Turning, she faced him. "I'm ready."

He fingered a tendril of her hair that curled along her cheek. "Then let's go have some fun."

Nick had chosen a restaurant in the center of Burlington. As he drove, they talked about the progress on the scenery for the pageant and his ideas for his new store. Every once in a while, he would glance at her and, even in the shadows, she could feel the heat of his gaze.

After they parked, he came around the car and helped her out, holding her elbow as they walked over icy patches. It felt right being close to Nick... touching...talking. He'd come to bed late every night this week to make sleeping together easier. But she suspected he had expectations for tonight, and to be honest with herself, she did, too.

The restaurant was divided into a dining area and a section set up with the band and a more casual atmosphere. Amid the crystal, silver and brass chandeliers, Faith could feel the elegance and see that Nick was completely at home—from tipping the maître d' so he'd put them at a quiet table, to ordering from a menu with prices that Faith normally wouldn't even consider paying for food.

She and Nick talked through dinner—about the excellent food, Christmas presents she wanted to buy for Jakie, her parents' porch. As the waiter brought coffee, she wondered where the time had gone.

When music started in the adjoining room, Nick nodded to it. "Are you game for dancing?"

"If you promise not to groan if I step on your toes. It's been awhile," she admitted.

Nick rose and pulled out her chair. "It's like riding a bicycle. You never forget. Having the right partner helps, too," he murmured close to her ear.

Shivers slipped down her spine.

They chose a table near the edge of the parquet

dance floor. They hadn't ordered drinks at dinner and now Faith was surprised when Nick ordered a mineral water with lime. She asked for a cranberry spritzer.

"If you want to drink something stronger, I can drive home."

He shook his head. "It's not necessary."

"Because of your dad?" she asked, not wanting to pry, but wanting to know everything there was to know about her husband.

"Because of my dad. Even as a kid, I made the choice never to end up like him...never to let someone or something else control my destiny."

She thought about the rumors she'd heard in high school about the gang Nick hung out with...the parties. He must have read her mind because he said, "I dumped a lot of beer...along the highway...into plants. I ran with the crowd, but I made my own rules."

"Did anyone know?" She realized how lonely Nick must have been.

"Bud did. He was the only one."

Into the momentary silence a new song played. Nick stood and offered Faith his hand. She took it and let him lead her to the dance floor.

As the music wound around them, as other couples joined them on the dance floor, Nick didn't hesitate to take Faith into his arms and bring her close. His hand enveloped hers and he brought it into his chest. He guided their movement so effortlessly, she felt as if she were floating in a dream rather than dancing.

"You always smell so good," he murmured close to her temple.

She leaned back, studying the clean-shaven line of his jaw, his firm, well-shaped lips, his intent blue eyes. She couldn't help but want to touch him, to truly belong to him, to fulfill every promise she'd made in her wedding vows, because she'd fallen head over heels in love with him. Each new day deepened feelings that had begun years ago—a crash that had bloomed into so much more. "I'm glad you suggested a night out."

When he bent his head, she knew he was going to kiss her, right there on the dance floor, and she didn't care. Before his lips touched hers, he whispered, "The night's not over yet."

Nick's lips were seductive, his tongue coaxing. But she didn't need to be coaxed. She met the forays of his tongue with strokes of her own. Her fingers kneaded his shoulder as she tried to ground herself, touch more of him, delve into the heat that had begun as small flames and were now licking at her, trying to consume her. Nick could so easily become essential to her world and she was still afraid to let that happen. Yet the fire burning between them told her she might not have any choice.

Her own desire compelled Faith to give Nick what he wanted. She lifted her arms, locking her hands behind his neck and pressed into him, her nipples rubbing against his suit jacket. They grew hard and her arms trembled. Nick continued their slow, sinuous body movement along with the kiss. He stopped to take a breath, to gaze into her eyes, then nibbled her lower lip and sucked it into his mouth. When she pressed even closer, she felt the ridge of his arousal.

The evidence of his desire made her feel proud, and needed, and much more sure of herself. When Nick's large hand slid up her waist to the side of her breast, she didn't consider propriety or her doubts about their hasty marriage. His touch was exciting and new and an intimacy she craved.

She felt his deep sigh as he pulled back. "We'd better slow this down or they'll throw us off the dance floor." Putting a few inches between them, he gave her a smile that kept her pulse galloping.

As the music ended, Nick guided her to their table. But as he pulled out her chair, she said, "I'm going to freshen up."

He fingered her earlobe. "Hurry back. The night's still young."

Faith found the ladies room, aware of his smile and bubbling with happy feelings, as she touched up her lipstick and made sure every strand of her hair was in place. She felt pretty tonight—pretty enough to turn Nick's head.

After she finished in the bathroom, she walked down the hall. The music had a faster beat now and the dance area was dark, lit only by the glimmers of a revolving strobe light. Taking a moment to get her bearings, she looked for their table. As the white light glimmered off the wall, she saw Nick.

Standing.

Talking to a woman—a woman dressed in a short, short gold lamé dress with a neckline that practically dipped to her waist.

He smiled at her, cocked his head and looked very interested. Then he laughed and wrote something on a business card, handing it to her. She took it and slipped it into the V of her neckline. For safekeeping, Faith supposed, wondering if Nick's gaze had followed the woman's hand. Telling herself not to jump to conclusions, Faith put one foot in front of the other and crossed to the table. But before she could reach her husband, the other woman moved away.

She came up behind him and laid her hand on his arm. "An old friend?"

Nick turned toward her. "Not exactly. She's a sales rep from one of the companies I buy from."

It was a plausible explanation. She might have felt better about it if the woman hadn't been so attractive.

Before she could sit again in the chair Nick pulled out, a voice came over the speaker system. "If Faith Clark is here, she can take a call at the hostess's station."

Faith's heart pounded. "Only my parents know where we are."

With a motion toward the hostess's desk, Nick said, "Let's find out what's going on."

He followed Faith, wondering if her mother had interrupted their evening intentionally. Because he had no doubt that it was Constance on the phone. The evening had been going so well. Until Faith had returned from the ladies room and seen him talking to Kathleen. The uncertainty had reappeared in her eyes. She had no need to feel uncertain. She looked beautiful tonight. Not that he didn't always find her beautiful. Her gentleness and caring wrapped around his heart until he felt almost new.

He'd intended to take her to bed tonight, no doubt about that. Her signals and responses had told him she'd be more than willing. But as he watched her pick up the phone and he saw the concerned expression on her face, he knew their plans for the night were about to change.

After she listened for a few minutes, she said, "Put him on."

"What's wrong, honey? Jakie, try to stop crying and listen to me. We'll be there in a half hour. I promise.

Have Grandma show you the clock. We'll come get you and bring you home.''

When Faith hung up, she turned to Nick. "He doesn't want to stay there overnight. He's afraid if he does, we won't come get him tomorrow.''

Realizing Constance's call had been necessary, Nick's annoyance with Faith's mother vanished. ''I'll get our coats.''

The drive back to Winding Creek was silent as Nick remembered his own turmoil as a child. His mother had told his father she'd be back after some time away...after she thought about what she wanted. But she hadn't meant it. She'd lied. After the night she'd left, they'd never heard from her again. Nick's greatest fear as a young boy was that his father would leave the way his mother had. As he'd gotten older, he'd decided to become tough enough and independent enough that it didn't matter. His father had stayed...physically, but had never been available emotionally till he got sober.

"We should have foreseen this," Nick said into the darkness. "We should have realized how insecure Jakie still is. You're his rock, Faith. And the thought of you not being there...''

"I'll reassure him. He'll see that we *did* come back. Eventually he'll learn to trust us.''

Trust was such a fragile thing. He and Pam might have worked out a viable marriage even as young as they were. But her lie...her deception...had made it impossible for Nick to ever trust her again. With trust gone, they'd had nowhere to go.

As soon as Faith stepped inside the door of her mother's house, Jakie ran to her and held on tight. Constance brought him his coat, Tom patted his head and Nick helped him zip and button. But the five-year-old returned to Faith and wouldn't let go of her hand. Not then. Not when they arrived at home.

Nick unlocked the door, and Faith took Jakie upstairs, with a glance over her shoulder that said, first and foremost, she had to take care of Jakie. Going to the kitchen, Nick poured a glass of milk and took two cookies from the cookie jar. He couldn't do much for the five-year-old, but he could remind him this was home.

Milk and cookies in hand, Nick climbed the stairs, and when he reached the top, he heard Jakie ask Faith, "Can you sleep with me tonight?"

Stopping at the door to the little boy's room, Nick watched Faith as she crouched down beside him. "I'm not going anywhere, honey. Our room is right across the hall."

"I know. But I want you to sleep with me and Teddy."

Faith raised her head and saw Nick standing at the door. He could tell she was torn about what to do...what was best to do.

Nick set the glass of milk and cookies on the nightstand and sank down on the bed. Then he beckoned to Jakie and patted his leg.

After a glance at Faith, Jakie slowly approached Nick. Nick lifted him onto his lap. "How about...just for tonight...all three of us sort of camp out in here? You can sleep in your bed, and Faith and I will bunk on the floor."

Jakie broke into a smile. "All of us?"

"All of us. Now, you eat your cookies and drink your milk while Faith and I get everything we need."

"An' brush my teeth again?"

Faith answered him this time. "That would be a very good idea."

Leaving Jakie on his bed with his cookies, Nick and Faith went into the hall. Outside the room, Faith said in a low voice, "I'm sorry tonight didn't turn out as we expected."

Nick wanted to tug her into his arms and kiss her until morning. But knowing in a short while they'd be sleeping together in less space than their bed, he knew a kiss would be a very unwise idea. "We married because of Jakie and now we have to make him feel secure. But we have to set boundaries, too."

"What if he wants us to sleep with him every night?"

"We'll cross that bridge when we get to it. But I think tonight will show him we aren't going anywhere. Bringing him home from your parents' was the right decision. He knows we're here for him."

"Thank you, Nick. For understanding."

Her soft brown eyes and the sweet curve of her lips tempted Nick to think about his own needs rather than Jakie's. But he forced desire to the farthest corner of his mind. "I understand Jakie's fears. That's why I want to make him feel secure as much as you do."

Faith's grateful smile and the feelings it invoked in him made him realize once again this could be a very long night.

A half hour later, Nick settled on the stack of quilts and covers beside Faith in the dark, though the night-light still glowed in the hall. The space where they'd laid the bedclothes was smaller than a double bed. There was no way he could get through the night without touching Faith or without her brushing against him.

"Night, Nick," Jakie called from his bed.

"Good night, champ."

"Night, Faith."

"Good night, honey."

Faith was lying on her side, facing Jakie's bed, to give Nick as much room as possible. But he was too tall and his shoulders too broad to settle in easily. Finally, he gave up the idea of trying to keep any space between them. Torture was torture so he might as well be comfortable while he endured it. Turning on his side, he wrapped his arm around Faith's waist.

Then he whispered into her ear, "Is that all right?"

He felt her nod.

Lying there with her, his body didn't understand his mind's directions—to pretend she wasn't a soft, beautiful woman he desired. He was aroused, and when Faith shifted, he knew she knew it.

"Nick?"

"It's okay. Go to sleep." As he breathed in her scent, he thought about his apartment back in Rutland, the nights he'd slept alone.

And frustration didn't seem to be such torture after all.

Chapter Eight

When the phone rang, Faith awakened, instantly aware of her body snuggled close to Nick's, her head on his shoulder, her hand lying familiarly on his bare chest. He was still asleep. She slid from under the covers and noticed Jakie was still sleeping, too. As quietly as she could, she hurried down the hall and grabbed the phone in the office expecting the caller to be her mother. Constance Hewitt thought everyone rose at seven a.m.

Usually she did. But she and Nick hadn't been sleeping very well, and last night... She smiled. She'd slept wonderfully.

Picking up the phone, she said, "Hi, Mom."

The deep clearing of a voice told her it wasn't her mother.

"This is Greg Blumfield. Could I speak to Nicholas Clark."

"Oh, I'm sorry. He's not up yet. This is his wife. Can I take a message?"

There was a pause. "His wife? I didn't know he was... Well, uh, Mrs. Clark, I'm his manager at The Toy Station. He arranged for a shipment to be delivered to the community center in Winding Creek today. I wanted to make sure someone would be there to receive the merchandise."

It was a lot to absorb in the minutes after awakening. But one piece of information stood out in bold relief—Nick hadn't told the manager of his store that he'd married.

"Wait just a moment and I'll get him."

As she walked down the hall, she vividly remembered the picture at the restaurant last night of Nick handing his card to a pretty blonde. *Was* she simply a sales rep? Maybe he was hedging his bets in case this marriage didn't work out. Or to get his physical needs met. Why hadn't he told his manager that he'd married? Because it might only be temporary?

At the doorway, she saw Nick wrestling with Jakie on the bedroll. He was tickling the five-year-old and Jakie was giggling. The scene usually would have filled her with joy but right now it just made her heart ache. How would Jakie feel if Nick left?

"It's for you," she said above Jakie's giggles.

Nick propped on his elbow.

"It's your manager."

A shadowed look passed over Nick's face.

"Apparently he didn't know we were married," she added.

"Faith..."

"Would you like scrambled eggs or pancakes for breakfast?"

Climbing to his feet, he frowned. "It doesn't matter what we have for breakfast, Faith. It *does* matter that we talk. I'll only be a few minutes." He passed her with a look that said she'd better be there when he got off the phone.

Faith helped Jakie dress and when he asked if he could watch a favorite Saturday morning cartoon, she agreed. Trying not to think, but most of all trying not to feel, she took the sheet from their bedroll and folded it. When Nick reentered the room, she kept folding.

"Have you told everyone you know that we're married?" he asked.

"This is Winding Creek. I didn't have to say a word."

Coming into the room, he reached for the blanket and folded it quickly. "I was going to tell Greg after I got plans going for the new store. I didn't want rumors starting. I didn't want anyone to think I'm going to sell out in Rutland and leave our employees without jobs."

"So…you didn't tell him because if he thought you were settling in Winding Creek he might fear losing his job? When you're planning to open a second store in Burlington? That doesn't make sense, Nick."

He flopped the blanket on the bed. "I didn't tell Greg I was scouting locations for a second store. He thinks I'm taking a longer vacation."

"Why?" she asked, even more dismayed. It was as if Nick was hiding his life with her and Jakie. Maybe he wasn't sure about opening a store in Burlington because he wasn't sure he was going to stay.

"Greg's been my manager for a year. An excellent one. But you know what rumors are like in Winding Creek. It's the same among employees. If I told Greg I got married, was adopting a child and moving here, and was thinking about opening a store in Burlington, it might have thrown him for a loop. For the time being, at least until after the new year, I just wanted to avoid gossip and problems.''

Faith heard what Nick was saying and could see his logic, yet she still wondered about his motivation. Maybe he wasn't sure yet he wanted to *be* married. "So you didn't tell anyone for business reasons.''

"Yes.''

"But now Greg knows.''

"He knows, but he swore he'd keep all of it under his hat until I firm up plans for the new store and can show the employees something concrete. I hope I convinced him this change for me won't affect him or the other employees. I don't want him looking for a job elsewhere and quitting this time of year.''

"So if anyone calls, I shouldn't tell them we're married.''

Nick rubbed the back of his neck. "It's not a secret. And no one but Greg will be calling. Don't make this into a major crisis, Faith. It's not.''

Backing away from him, hurt he was treating the situation so lightly, she said, "Fine. It's not a major crisis. I'll remember that when someone I don't know calls and I have to think twice about telling them we're married.'' She scooped up the rest of the bedroll and laid it on Jakie's bed. "I'll take care of this later. I have practice at the center with the kids at ten. By the way, your manager mentioned something about a delivery today to the community center. Anything I should know about?''

"I'm having toys shipped in for the Christmas party tomorrow. Some stuffed toys, cars and trucks, dolls. And before you tell me that they're not in the budget, I'm donating them.''

Surprised for a moment, she didn't know what to say. "Thank you."

They gazed at each other for a short while in silence, tension and sexual sparks vibrating between them. Faith remembered how she'd awakened in his arms, feeling close to him...

She broke eye contact and moved toward the door. "Faith?"

When she turned, he said, "Not telling my manager...it *was* just business."

Without responding, she went down the hall to her room, wishing she could believe him, but knowing in her heart she didn't.

The evergreen was about eight feet tall and Nick hoped it would fit into their living room. Actually what he hoped was that it would light up Faith's eyes again when she looked at him.

Always expect the unexpected, he reminded himself as he dragged the fir tree from the trunk of his car and carried it up the walk. He'd never expected Greg to talk to Faith; he'd never expected Faith to be so upset. And she was. He could tell from the way she avoided his gaze, the way she'd kept busy at the center without coming near him as he'd unloaded the toys from the truck when it had arrived.

The truth was—he didn't know how to go about mending fences. She must think that he was ashamed of their marriage or at least the way they got married, and that wasn't true at all. Their situation was just...complicated.

She and Jakie had left the center before Nick had finished unpacking the toys. When all the children had left, he'd tried on the Santa suit. That red outfit and fake white whiskers had given him the best feeling, and that's when he'd decided to bring some Christmas spirit home.

When he opened the front door, the smell of baked goods drifted out. He breathed in deeply, then took the tree inside. Jakie saw him first and hopped up and down with excitement. "Look, Faith. A Christmas tree. Can we decorate it now?"

Faith came into the living room, a bib apron covering her pale blue sweater and jeans. "You'll have to ask Nick," she said softly. "I don't know if he's going to set it up right away."

Nick propped the tree against the wall. "That depends. If you have a tree stand, I'll set it up now."

"It's in the closet in the office. If you wait until I take the cookies out of the oven..."

"Jakie and I can get it. Unless you'd like us to wait."

"No. It should be on the left. It's labeled. There's a box under it with decorations and lights. Just bring it all down and we'll find what we need."

At least she looked pleased. At least she hadn't told him to take the tree and shove it. At least she might be open to mending fences.

Putting up the tree took longer than Nick planned until he made sure it was straight in the stand, until they decided where to put it, until he wrapped and tucked white twinkle lights around the branches and laced gold beads over the boughs. When they took a break for supper, Faith was much quieter than usual, but Jakie's excitement over the Christmas preparations and the party the next day filled in the awkward silences.

After eating a few of the oatmeal-raisin cookies Faith

had baked for the party, Nick said, "You'll have to show me what you want on the top of the tree. We should put that on first."

Faith laid her napkin on the table. "I know exactly where it is. Mom gave it to me when I bought the house."

"Can we get it now?" Jakie asked with that magic sparkle in his eyes that Christmas usually ignited in children.

When Faith stood, she smiled. "Sure. We can let the dishes sit."

She headed straight for a green carton and knelt down beside it. Jakie sat on the floor beside her. After she removed the lid, she picked up a white box in the corner. Offering it to Jakie, she let him open it.

He pushed back the tissue paper much more carefully than Nick would have expected, as if he knew he was unwrapping something important. "It's an angel!"

"Go ahead and take her out of the box," Faith encouraged him.

The angel was created out of a papier-mâché type substance and was painted in rich shades of burgundy and emerald green. A gold halo sat atop her head. Jakie reverently fingered the golden wings.

"When Mom gave her to me, she said she hoped she would bring me Christmas blessings for many, many years."

Nick heard the huskiness in Faith's voice and realized how much the gift had meant to her. He also saw the look she bestowed on Jakie, and he knew she was thinking he was the greatest blessing of all. She glanced up at Nick and he saw gratitude for helping her keep the boy she wanted as a son.

But he wanted more than gratitude.

Jakie said, "I got wings but not one of these." He poked at the halo. "Can we make them, too?"

Faith laughed. "We have ten days till Christmas Eve. I think we can manage a few halos."

"You're comin' to the pageant. Right, Nick?"

"I wouldn't miss it," he assured Jakie, finally realizing why the idea of skipping Christmas was unimaginable to Faith.

Nick had never decorated a Christmas tree. His father had never bothered with them. He and Pam hadn't been married long enough to share a Christmas. And a bachelor alone on Christmas didn't need a tree. Jakie was entranced by the shiny balls, the miniature houses, the wooden rocking horse and reindeer. And so was Nick.

When Jakie hung the last ornament, they stood back and admired their work. Nick plugged in the lights and Jakie gave a small gasp. Nick's throat tightened and as he gazed at Faith, he saw her eyes glisten. He so much wanted to take her in his arms, but she looked away and hooked her arm around Jakie's shoulders. "Time to get your pj's on."

The smile slid from Jakie's face. "Are you and Nick gonna sleep in my room tonight?"

Faith crouched down before him. "You have your room to sleep in and we have ours. But tonight, you can leave your door open and we'll leave our door open. If you need to make sure we're there, you just call. Okay?"

He bobbed his head. "But can you camp out in my room again? Soon?"

"What about after Christmas?" Nick suggested. "And maybe sometime you could ask one of your friends to come over and camp out with you."

"Can I, Faith?"

"Sure. I bet George Matson would come over if you ask him."

"Can I ask him tomorrow?"

"I'll call his mom. Maybe he can just come home with us after the Christmas party."

"Wow! Are you gonna call her now?"

"Okay, but you go get ready for bed while I do."

With his usual enthusiasm Jakie raced up the steps.

As Faith rose to her feet, Nick approached her. "Good ideas take on a momentum of their own."

"Think you can handle an afternoon of playing Saint Nick and two five-year-olds having a sleepover?"

He laughed. "Saint Nick?"

As she shrugged, she said, "The title seems to fit. You married me to protect Jakie. You donated the toys for tomorrow."

Nick wasn't used to sarcasm coming from Faith and he didn't hear it now. But there was a quality to her voice that kept distance between them. Trying to eliminate it, he reached out and caressed her cheek. "You and I both know I'm no saint."

She trembled when his fingers touched her skin, but after a moment of acute awareness, she backed away. "I have to call Margie. Jakie will want a full report when he comes down."

When Faith went to the telephone, he knew they'd be sleeping on separate sides of the bed tonight. Faith might have appreciated the Christmas tree, but she hadn't forgotten what had happened earlier.

How long would it take?

The children gathered around Nick on Sunday afternoon as he listened to their Christmas wishes, now and then taking signals from their parents. Faith had noted from the moment he'd appeared in the red suit that he made a great St. Nick. His booming ho-ho's filled the room every now and then and he played his character to the hilt.

If she hadn't been so upset yesterday about him not telling his associates about their marriage, it would have been a wonderful day. Nick had taken such pride in the Christmas tree as if it was the first one he'd ever had. His enthusiasm had been catching and, for a little while, she'd felt they were a real family and almost trusted him to stay. But then doubts had cropped up again. Especially as they lay on separate sides of the bed.

Suddenly Faith's mother appeared by her side with a decorative tin of cookies and opened it on the table where Faith was ladling cider into paper cups. "He's good with children," she said, taking the lid from the tin.

"He's wonderful with Jakie," Faith offered, wondering where her mother was headed. She didn't usually comment without making a point.

"I heard he donated all the toys for today. We've only ever given oranges and candy canes before."

"I guess Nick wanted to do something special."

It must have been the opening her mother was waiting for. "And what happens next year if he's not here? These children will be disappointed..."

"Mother, don't you think Nick will want to stay? Don't you think I can make him happy?"

"Honey, you can't *make* another person happy. They have to do that all on their own."

"Nick's a good man."

Her mother was pensive for a moment. "Maybe he

is. He didn't have to help us with our roof. And he didn't have to put all that work into the scenery."

"And he didn't have to volunteer to play Santa," Faith added softly, watching him hold a little girl on his knee the way he often held Jakie when he read him a story.

Constance took Faith's arm. "Is he being kind to you? I mean, he's not being demanding, is he?"

Faith's cheeks flared and so did her usually placid temper. "That's enough, Mom. I won't discuss the details of our marriage with you." Not that there were many details to discuss. She wasn't about to admit that Nick hadn't even told his manager in Rutland about their marriage. That would only fuel her mother's doubts.

"I'm worried about you, Faith. About Jakie."

"We're doing fine. We have another interview with Darla tomorrow night."

"I imagine the Brewers will have another one soon, too."

When Faith thought about the Brewers, she got cold inside. But she had every reason to be hopeful. "Probably. We have to go over all the worksheets with Darla that we filled out, give her our income tax returns." Not wanting to answer more questions or field them, Faith asked, "Can you handle the food? I'm going to get more toys for Nick to hand out."

Several people stopped Faith as she made her way to Nick. George and Jakie had already sat on Nick's lap and were now playing with their toy trucks under Margie and Bud's supervision. Margie looked tired. Taking George off her hands for tonight might help. Two women in the pageant confirmed the time of the next practice. A few others congratulated Faith on her recent marriage. All of them filled Faith with a sense of belonging. Yet as she picked up a stack of toys and set them beside Nick's chair, his gaze met hers and she wanted to feel an entirely different sense of belonging.

After Nick had asked the last child what she wanted for Christmas and handed the little girl a small stuffed bear, Jakie came up to him and stared at him for a few moments.

Faith asked, "What's wrong, Jakie?"

"You're not Santa. You're Nick."

Nick gathered Jakie onto his lap and murmured close to his ear, "Santa couldn't be here today so I thought I'd take his place. Did I do a good job?"

Jakie nodded. "But Santa's comin' Christmas Eve, right?"

"I'm positive he is. Are you sure you don't want anything besides a fire engine?" Nick asked.

Faith had heard Jakie make his request earlier. Fortunately she'd already bought one, and it was tucked in the corner of her closet.

"I *do* want somethin' else."

Faith and Nick listened closely.

"I want Faith to be my mom and I want you to be my dad."

Faith wasn't sure how to answer with the Brewers in the picture and she and Nick still finding their way.

After Nick cleared his throat, he said, "I'll talk to Santa about it and see what we can do."

"Promise?" the five-year-old asked.

"Promise," Nick assured him.

Stretching his arms around Nick's neck, Jakie hugged him hard.

Tears burned Faith's eyes and she blinked them away. If only they could become a *real* family.

A short time later, now devoid of his Santa suit, Nick drove them home. But when he pulled up at the house, another car sat in front of it, one Faith didn't recognize. Nick parked his behind it. When she and the boys hopped out, she recognized the woman emerging from the car with her curly blond hair, slender figure in her long forest green wool coat, and tempting smile.

A sales rep, huh? Visiting Nick on a Sunday at his home. That didn't sound like business to Faith. She pictured the easy expression on Nick's face when he'd handed the woman his card, his smile that could charm a girl into dreaming about him. She thought about his virile appeal and the nights they'd spent in bed not touching. And she knew he needed a lot more.

In her insulated jacket and jeans, with her hair disheveled around her earmuffs, Faith decided her best strategy was to retreat. Without saying a word, she guided George and Jakie up the walk at a fast clip and went inside. She thought she heard Nick call her name, but she didn't open the door again to find out.

Faith's heart pounded as Jakie took George up to his room to show him his favorite cars. She followed with George's backpack, trying not to think about Nick and another woman talking outside—maybe making plans to do more than talk. Seeing George and Jakie settled on the floor of his room, happily running the miniature cars and trucks across the floor, she went downstairs to start supper.

She'd started browning meat to make tacos when she heard the front door open and close. Two minutes later, Nick stood in the kitchen, the sleeves of his flannel shirt rolled to his elbows, his jeans much too snug for her peace of mind.

"Why did you come racing in here?" he asked, his voice gruff.

She kept stirring. "I had to get the boys settled. Besides, I didn't think the two of you wanted company."

Nick reached around her and switched off the burner on the stove. "Explain that."

Impatiently she flicked the switch on again. "Nick, I have to finish this and get it simmering—"

This time, he took the spatula from her hand, set it on the range and turned the burner's switch with a determined click. "The boys filled up on cookies. They're probably not hungry. And you and I have something to finish before we can even think about supper. Tell me what you're thinking."

Angry now that she felt so vulnerable and defensive, she gave him what he wanted. "I'm thinking you want that sales rep, if she *is* a sales rep, to be more than a sales rep. I'm thinking you gave her your number the other night for more than business reasons. I'm thinking she looks like all the cheerleaders you used to date!"

She couldn't tell if anger or desire flared in Nick's eyes, and she didn't have time to analyze it because he yanked her into his arms and kissed her with an intensity that drove every thought from her mind.

His chest was hard against her breasts, his hands firm on her back. When his tongue drove into her mouth, her nipples grew hard and she instinctively rubbed against him. Nick groaned and he rocked his hips against hers, igniting fire in her womb. It spread through her fast, making her burn for him...with him. She clutched his shoulders and breathed in the scent of him—cold air and Nick.

His hands abandoned his hold on her and moved

down, grasping the hem of her sweater. She was too intoxicated by his kiss to think about what he was doing or even care. But when his rough fingers touched her bare skin, the sensation was so exquisite she could only curl her fingers into his shoulders and wish the kiss would never end.

All of a sudden, he lifted her onto the counter, then cupped her head, still kissing her as if it was the first, last and only kiss they'd ever share. Nick's urgency and lack of restraint excited and aroused her so completely that she didn't know herself as she wantonly kissed him back, stroking her tongue against his, caressing his back, exploring, needing to know more of him.

He was solid, he was a fantasy come true, he was her husband and she loved him. He was overwhelming her with a pure sensuality and pleasure she'd never imagined. As he ravaged her mouth, he released her head. She missed the heat of his hands, the grounding, the stability of him surrounding her.

Then suddenly, his fingers lifted her sweater again and danced across her midriff. When his hand cupped her breast, she ached in a way that seemed too deep, and dark, and forbidden to ever fulfill. The ache became an excruciating longing as he unhooked her bra with one hand and flicked the cotton out of the way with the other.

As the kiss went on and on, the anticipation of his touch urged her to arch into his hand. The waiting was too difficult...too unnecessary. Nick grazed his thumb over her nipple and she moaned. He did it again, and she slid her hands up his neck into his hair, ruffling it, relishing it, trying to make him understand she needed more of everything.

As he kneaded her breast, she knew what she wanted, but didn't know how to get it. He was standing between her legs and she slid closer to him, squeezing her knees against his hips.

Nick was too far gone to be gentle or coaxing. The frustration and anger that had ignited the kiss had long passed, leaving pure desire in its wake. The torture of lying next to Faith night after night, wanting her, needing her, yet knowing he couldn't touch her until she wanted and needed him just as much was driving him crazy. This stupid situation today with her jumping to all the wrong conclusions had been the drop of water that had made the pitcher overflow.

Faith was the sweetest woman he'd ever met—the most caring, the most honest. But her doubts about herself, her doubts about him, were getting in their way. If he could just reach her with the passion between them...

A thump on the ceiling distracted him for a moment. A second thump reminded him that as much as he wanted to make love to Faith right here, right now, there were two small boys upstairs who needed supervision.

He tore away from Faith, taking a deep breath, trying to rein in the raging desire.

"Nick...?"

Faith's eyes were as passion-glazed as he was sure his were. He shook his head and held up his hand, steadying his breathing, willing his pulse to slow and his libido to cool down.

"I heard something upstairs," he finally managed to say.

"Jakie and George."

Faith's voice was shaky and he understood the feeling.

With her cheeks bright rose, her lips just-kissed, Faith clasped her bra and pulled down her sweater. "It's probably good they're up there—"

"Why? So you don't have to face the passion between us? Damn it, Faith. Kathleen *is* a sales rep. She told me the other night she had catalogues for a new line of toys. When she learned I was staying in Winding Creek, she said she'd drop them off on her way to Rutland. That's why I gave her a card with the address."

"She could have left them at the door," Faith murmured, finally meeting his gaze.

He could still hear the doubt, and anger rose to the surface again. "She would have, but we pulled up as she was checking the house number. Tell me something, Faith. How are we supposed to have a marriage if you don't trust me?"

Jumping down from the counter, Faith stood straight-backed before him. "How can I trust you when you didn't even tell your friends that we're married?"

Guilt stabbed Nick and he realized much of this misunderstanding was his own fault. That realization didn't keep him from feeling defensive. "I don't have friends in Rutland. Not like you have here. I told you why I didn't tell my manager, but you'd rather believe I have some ulterior motive. I wish you'd believe in yourself, Faith. I wish you'd believe in me."

When Nick heard a third clunk upstairs, he said, "I'd better check on them." He waited for Faith to stop him. He waited for her to say she could believe in herself and him. But she didn't.

Frustrated with himself, frustrated with her, he strode through the living room and up the stairs.

Chapter Nine

A hot glue gun and wire forms sat on the table between Faith and Margie as they created wreaths for the community center from pine cones, ribbon and evergreen boughs. They had finished three large ones and had started smaller ones.

"This was a great idea, Faith. It's easier to watch George and Jakie here rather than at the center. The twins are going to a neighbor's when they get home from school, so I don't have to worry about rushing back." Margie patted the cushion on the seat of the chair. "Much more comfortable here, too, than those folding chairs." After she rubbed the small of her back, she said, "I hope George behaved last night."

"He's good for Jakie. They had fun."

"Did you and Nick get any sleep?" Margie asked with a knowing smile.

Her and Nick. In the kitchen. Their kiss. His touch. The tension between them that they'd tried to ignore as they played games with the boys, set up the futon in Jakie's room for George, then listened to the five-year-olds' voices long after midnight. Jakie had called out to them about three a.m. He'd just wanted to know they were there.

"Some," Faith answered with a forced smile, remembering the rigidity of her body in the bed, the echo of Nick's words that she was running away from the passion between them. Shifting on her chair, she glanced into the living room where the boys were coloring.

"You know, if Jakie likes having another child around, maybe you and Nick will have to do something about it," her friend said with a wink.

"I think it's a little early for that."

Examining Faith closely, Margie asked, "Is everything all right between the two of you?"

Faith wanted to blurt out the whole story—how Nick had married her because of Jakie, how he'd left for Burlington this morning to meet a real estate agent and told her he'd be back in time for their meeting with Darla without his usual gentleness, with a remoteness that almost scared her. But everyone was supposed to think she and Nick were happily married newlyweds so she kept her turmoil to herself.

Straightening her spine, she plumped the gold bow she'd tied while they talked and answered with, "We're still adjusting to marriage."

As a comforting gesture, Margie patted Faith's arm. "Even after all these years, Bud and I still— Oh!"

Margie's gasp startled Faith. "What is it?"

"My water broke. Oh my gosh. Oooh..." Margie's face tightened in pain and she held her arms over her belly.

Faith's chair almost overturned as she jumped up. "Let's get you to the hospital."

Panting through the contraction Margie shook her head. "No time to get to Burlington. Short labor for both deliveries. I should have known the back pain that started this morning wasn't just back pain. And the pangs I've been having for the last few hours weren't false labor..." Her voice slid into a moan as another contraction hit. "Send the boys upstairs," she managed to say through clenched teeth.

The reality of having to deliver a baby hit Faith and she moved quickly, trying to recall details of a first aid and emergency care class she'd taken last year at the community center. Making some excuse to the boys about needing to spread out Christmas decorations in the living room, she asked them to play in Jakie's room till supper. Without giving her request any resistance, they gathered markers, crayons and pictures and scrambled upstairs.

Just as Faith made sure they'd gone down the hall, the front door opened and Nick came in.

"Thank goodness," Faith breathed. "Margie's in labor. Will you call 911 while I get her on the sofa?"

With a fast assessment, hearing the boys upstairs and seeing Margie bent over in pain on the chair, Nick shed his jacket. "I don't know how soon the ambulance will get here. It's snowing again and a tractor trailer jack-knifed across the road to Burlington. I had to take a long detour to get home. Why don't you call 911. I'll get Margie to the sofa."

Realizing he could handle her friend better than she could, Faith ran for the phone.

"Phone Bud, too," Nick called after her. "He might still be at school."

In the kitchen, Faith made the calls, grabbing towels from a drawer and a kettle from the cupboard. If Margie's labor was short and the ambulance didn't get here in time, they'd have no choice but to deliver this baby. Filling the kettle with water, she put it on to boil and dropped a pair of scissors in to the water. As she remembered something else from the emergency care class, she found a ball of string in her miscellaneous drawer, snipped off two pieces and took it with her to the living room along with the towels. She might need it to tie the umbilical cord.

While Nick turned away, Faith helped Margie remove her shoes and slacks between two very sharp contractions.

"Is there anything I can do to help?" he asked after Faith had covered Margie with the quilt. "Or do you want me to wait upstairs with the boys?"

"Don't leave on my account," Margie said then started panting again.

Faith knelt down beside her friend. "This could happen really fast and I might need your help. If you could stay…"

He approached Faith then and with a gentle look capped her shoulder. "Just tell me what you want me to do."

She wanted him to love her…really love her. Not because he needed a family, but because he wanted to be married to *her*. She knew they needed more time. She knew she had to be patient. She knew she had to learn to trust him. But for now, having him here was enough.

"See if the water's boiling. And dampen a towel so I can wipe her face." As he started to move away, she clasped his arm. When he gazed at her, his look was probing but the remoteness she'd seen in the morning was gone. Fighting her doubts, knowing she wanted her marriage to Nick to work more than she'd ever wanted anything in her life—except Jakie, she said, "I'm glad you're here."

He looked as if he wanted to say something, but as Margie almost sat up with the pain of the next contraction, he nodded and went to the kitchen.

A few minutes later, Bud rushed in the front door and took Faith's place on the floor beside his wife. "You're not due for another ten days. You're *always* late..."

"Tell that to this baby," Margie said with a smile that turned into a grimace.

Faith moved to the foot of the sofa as Bud took his wife's hand. Checking under the draped quilt, she calmed herself with a deep breath. "I can see the baby's head."

Bud's face went white. "Jeez, what are we going to do?"

"We're going to deliver this baby," Faith assured him, with more confidence than she felt, remembering the first rule of childbirth was to let nature take its course.

Faith had never felt part of anything as terrifying, as real, or as miraculous as what was happening before her. As Bud let his wife squeeze his hand, Margie pushed and Nick stood by Faith, ready to give her any assistance she needed.

As Margie bore down, Bud supported her physically and encouraged her emotionally. Faith could feel the bond between them...the hope...the love. The baby's head appeared, and she slipped her hands underneath its shoulders. Someday she wanted Nick beside her as

Bud was beside Margie. She wanted to be giving birth to Nick's child, seeing the wonder of a shared miracle in his eyes.

"With the next contraction, give a giant push," Faith said, her voice husky. Going on instinct, as well as the information she'd been taught, she knew if Margie put all her energy behind this next push, she'd have her baby in her arms. As the contraction took hold, Margie puffed up her cheeks and pushed with all her might.

The baby cried as Faith caught it and slipped a towel around it. "You have a girl," she said as her eyes filled with tears and she knew she'd remember this moment forever.

A siren screamed outside and lights flashed through the front windows. Moments later Nick was letting paramedics into the living room as Jakie and George ran down the steps. The living room was bedlam.

Faith laid Margie's little girl on her mother's stomach and let the paramedics take over. Bud smiled down at his daughter and kissed his wife long and hard. Then he went to the two wide-eyed little boys at the bottom of the steps.

Dropping his arm around George's shoulders, he said, "Now you have a sister."

"Can I see her?"

Bud took George's hand. "C'mon over here. Your mom and your sister have to go to the hospital and get checked out, but they'll be home in a day or two."

Kneeling down next to Jakie, Faith asked him, "Do you want to see the baby?"

He nodded his head and she led him to the gurney where the paramedics had settled Margie.

Margie took Faith's hand. "Thank you." She looked

behind Faith's shoulder at Nick. "You, too. Thank goodness I was with someone..." Her eyes glistened with tears.

"All in a day's work," Nick answered with a smile, but his voice was slightly husky and Faith could sense the birth of Bud and Margie's child had affected him, too.

"I do have another favor," Margie added. "Can George stay tonight? Bud's going to have his hands full with the twins..."

Faith glanced at Nick. Darla was coming. They wouldn't have any privacy later. Yet she couldn't let down a friend.

Nick answered for her. "It's not a problem."

Within the next fifteen minutes, the paramedics wheeled Margie and the baby out of the house. Then Bud hugged his son and told Faith he'd pick up George the following afternoon. Jakie and George gave each other high fives when they heard that they could spend the night together again. After they watched the ambulance drive away, Nick occupied them while Faith made dinner. There was no time to talk with the two boys taking their attention, asking questions, chattering about the ambulance and sirens and the new baby. They had just finished eating when the doorbell rang, and Faith felt as if she needed to take one very huge breath.

She quickly cleared the table while Nick answered the door. After settling the boys with a Christmas video in the living room, Faith and Nick sat across from Darla Granger at the kitchen table.

Before Darla could open her folder, Nick said, "Things are a bit chaotic. A friend had her baby here this afternoon and the boys are still wound up. They were upstairs when the baby was born—"

"She had her baby *here?*" Darla asked, astonished.

"There wasn't enough time to get her to the hospital," Faith explained calmly, telling herself every family had unusual occurrences. "It happened very fast and the boys didn't come down until it was over. Our friend's son is staying the night with Jakie."

"I see. As if Christmas doesn't bring enough excitement. So...tell me. In general how is everything going?"

When Faith glanced at Nick, he responded. "Faith and I went out for dinner last week, and Jakie was supposed to spend the night with Faith's mother. But we received a call at the restaurant because he didn't want to stay. He was afraid we wouldn't come back for him."

Darla's expression was neutral. "That's not surprising under the circumstances. How did you handle it?"

Faith explained how they'd "camped out" in Jakie's room.

"And whose idea was that?" Darla asked.

"It was mine," Nick admitted. "I don't know if it was the right thing to do, but I was concerned if Faith slept with Jakie, he'd want her there every night."

"And does he want the two of you on his floor every night?" the caseworker asked.

"We leave both doors open and we told him to call us whenever he wants to," Faith answered, knowing they had to be honest with Darla for Jakie's sake.

"It's hard to know if you've made the right decisions as parents. Only time will tell. When I talk to Jakie, I'll see how he's really feeling about all this. But what concerns me is the effect it's having on a new marriage. You two are getting some time alone, aren't you?"

Before Faith could think of an appropriate response, Nick did. "We had an enjoyable evening alone before the phone call. Dinner. Dancing. And as Jakie feels more secure, we'll have more privacy."

Darla looked from Faith to Nick, studying both of them for a moment. "Mr. Clark, you and Faith need to make time for privacy. I understand that Jakie is your main concern, and I applaud that. But this home-study will be as much about your marriage as it is about Jakie's needs. Now, why don't we go over those questionnaires I gave you and Faith to fill out. And I hope you have your income tax returns for me."

Nick slid a manila envelope across the table. "Everything is there that you asked for. Have the Brewers submitted all their paperwork?"

Darla opened the envelope and riffled through papers. "I can't discuss the Brewers with you, Mr. Clark. But I can tell you they are still interested in Jakie and want more visits. Apparently he struck a chord with them. But I've persuaded them to wait until after Christmas. That's all I can tell you until our evaluation is completed."

Frowning, Nick pushed. "If it were up to you, would you recommend Jakie stay with us?"

Faith's heart raced as she waited for the case-worker's answer.

Placing the papers on the table, Darla met Nick's gaze directly. "It's too early for me to say, even if I could. But I do see bonds forming among the three of you. I would like to see them strengthened, not broken."

Nick smiled and reached across the table for Faith's

hand. But she couldn't help but wonder if he did it simply for Darla's benefit or because they had truly formed a bond.

The following evening, Christmas carols blared from the boom box on the edge of the stage as Faith, her mother and a few other women decorated for the pageant. Practice had been very bumpy with many of the children not knowing their lines. But they still had eight days until Christmas Eve. One of the mothers was going over lines now, hoping repetition would help. Jakie stood with the group of children, listening for his cue. He didn't have a speaking part but he had to know when to climb the steps and appear.

Faith positioned the ladder to the side of the stage, intending to hang a large wreath on each side. She and Nick would finally have some time alone tonight after he went to bed. Provided Jakie went to sleep. Last night Jakie and George had been up and down throughout the night—going to the bathroom, getting drinks of water, giggling. She and Nick had lain on their respective sides of the bed...tossing, turning, aware of the boys right across the hall.

As Faith climbed the old ladder, she thought about what Darla had said about her and Nick needing private time. And they did. But since the snow had stopped after only having put down a few inches last night, Nick had gone into Burlington again this morning and he hadn't come home before she'd left for the center. After their tryst on the kitchen counter, she'd gotten the impression he was purposefully keeping his distance.

The ladder wobbled slightly as Faith climbed another step. It was rickety, but she knew she'd only be on it for another moment until she slipped the wire onto the nail...

One moment too long, she thought as the ladder tipped and she landed on the floor on her left side.

Her mother came rushing over. "Honey, are you all right?"

As other adults as well as the children gathered around her, Faith scrambled to her feet, a sharp pain stabbing her wrist. She looked squarely at Jakie. "I'm fine. Really." Glancing at the ladder that had collapsed, she noticed one of the metal brackets had torn from the side. "Do we have another ladder?"

Constance took Faith by the arm and waved everybody back to what they were doing. After practice resumed again, she asked in a low tone, "Don't you think you should sit down for a few minutes and make sure you're okay?"

"Mom, I'm fine. I just feel foolish." She stooped and picked up the twisted ladder, seeing that rusty screws holding the bracket onto the wood had caused her fall. But when she went to use her left hand, pain shot up her arm.

"What's wrong?" Constance asked, seeing her pull her hand back and hold it by her side.

"I must have bruised it. But it will be fine. I'll use ice when I get home. Go finish stringing popcorn. I'll look for another way to get that wreath hung."

The printer spewed out an inventory report as Nick took a cookie from the cookie jar on the counter. He'd found a great location for the store in a strip shopping center in Burlington. The real estate agent was ready to write up the papers for the lease. But he'd hesitated. He'd told her he wanted to sleep on it.

As if he was getting any sleep.

Ever since the other night in this kitchen, he'd known he had to stay away from Faith or he'd lose the tight grip he was holding on his desire. And ever since he'd witnessed the birth of Bud and Margie's baby, he'd been filled with the longing to have their kind of family. He smiled when he thought about four kids running around...

The phone rang and he answered it, still smiling.

"Nick, it's Faith's mother. Can you come down to the center?"

He glanced at the papers spread across the table, the data on the computer. "Is there a problem?"

"Faith fell off the ladder. She's pretending she's fine but she's not using her left hand and I'm afraid she broke something. That girl can be so stubborn sometimes—"

"I'll be right there. Don't let her try to drive home."

"I won't. And...thank you, Nick."

"No thanks necessary, Mrs. Hewitt. I'll be there in five minutes."

Without even shutting down the computer, Nick grabbed his jacket and headed for the door, furious with his wife. Why hadn't *she* called him? If she'd fallen from a ladder, she could be more injured than she thought.

Only a few cars were parked near the community center. Nick slid into a place, slammed his door and hurried inside. When he saw Faith, on a stepstool this time, trying to hang a wreath with one hand, he tried to put a lid on his anger, but it was damn difficult.

Standing at her elbow, he said, "Get down, Faith. Now."

"Nick, what are you doing here? Just a minute until I get this up…"

His patience long gone, he swept her up, wreath and all, and set her on the tile floor. Taking the wreath from her, he climbed onto the stool, hung the evergreens and hopped to the ground.

Then he pinned her with a hard stare. "Your mother called. She said you fell."

"I can't believe Mom called you!"

He noticed her cradling her hand. "Wiggle your fingers."

"Nick…"

"Wiggle your fingers," he ordered in a low but stern tone.

When she moved her fingers, she winced.

"Get your coat. I'm taking you to the Emergency Room."

"Don't be ridiculous. It's getting late to go into Burlington. We need to get Jakie to bed—"

He was so frustrated with her, he could shake her. Instead he firmly clasped her shoulders. "This is non-negotiable. You're getting that wrist and hand looked at tonight. I'm sure your mother will watch Jakie. Now, go find your coat." Before he kissed some sense into her, he released her and headed for Jakie.

Constance approached him and walked with him. "She's probably furious with me."

"I'm glad you called. She can hardly move her fingers and it looks swollen. Can you take Jakie home with you until we get back from the hospital?"

"Certainly, I can. But what if Jakie doesn't want to stay?"

When Jakie saw Nick, he left the circle of children and ran toward him. Nick crouched down in front of him at Jakie's eye level. "I need you to do me a favor, sport. Faith hurt her wrist when she fell and I'm going to take her to the doctor's. Will you go with Grandma and stay?"

The little boy looked uncertain.

"This is important, Jakie. I don't know how long we'll be, but I promise I'll come get you tonight. No matter how late it is."

"You promise?" Jakie asked.

"I promise," Nick assured him.

"We'll make hot chocolate and read some books," Constance offered.

"You won't forget?" Jakie asked Nick.

"I won't forget," Nick promised solemnly.

With that, the five-year-old nodded.

Nick didn't give Faith a chance to scold her mother for calling him. Once she saw Jakie wasn't upset about staying with Constance, she reassured him she'd be back as good as new and they'd come home as soon as they could. Then she let Nick hustle her out.

They drove to Burlington in silence. Nick suspected Faith was in more pain than she was letting on. Fortunately, it was a relatively quiet night in the ER. They didn't have to wait long until a doctor examined Faith and sent her for an X ray. Nick paced, agitated by more than Faith's injury.

Finally the doctor told them she'd sprained the wrist, not broken it. She should ice it for twenty-four hours and take acetaminophen for the pain.

On the way back to Winding Creek, Nick switched on the radio. Faith was probably thinking he'd created a brouhaha for no good reason. But sometimes a brouhaha was necessary.

When he reached the outskirts of Winding Creek and

headed for home rather than her mother's, she said, "We have to pick up Jakie."

"*I'm* going to pick up Jakie. *You're* going to get ice on that wrist," he snapped, still angry she wasn't thinking about what was best for her.

Faith didn't wait for him to help her out of the car, but she did let him unlock the door. Once inside, she shrugged off her coat. She hadn't zippered it, and she hadn't asked for his help. He took it from her now, hung it in the closet and closed the door with a snap.

"Nick, why are you so angry?"

Her soft voice, her beautiful brown eyes, the way she was holding her wrist pushed him past patience's boundaries. "Why am I angry? How about the fact that you're acting as if you're still single? I'm your husband, but you didn't even call me to let me know you were hurt, that you needed help."

"I didn't *need* help," she said pointedly, color bright in her cheeks. "I was going to come home and put ice on it. Mom should never have called you."

"And how would you have driven home? One-handed? Maybe you weren't concerned with your own safety but you should have been worried about Jakie's!"

"Don't you dare suggest I'd put Jakie in danger. It was only a few blocks. I didn't want to bother you if you were working."

Not being able to keep his distance, not being able to keep from touching her, he lifted her chin and demanded, "When are you going to put yourself first? When are you going to learn to take what you want?"

"Do you take what you want?" she asked, her gaze never wavering from his.

Desire, so hot and fast and strong, rushed through

him like a freight train. He dropped his hand. "Damn it, Faith. I want to sling you over my shoulder and carry you up those stairs and make you my wife in every sense of the word. But I know better than to take what you're not ready to give—"

"I am." She cut in, stopping him cold.

"You're what?" he asked, blood pounding at his temples and other more demanding places.

"I'm ready." Taking an obviously steadying breath, she went on, "I want to make love with you. But I didn't know how to tell you, and with George here..."

Her words registered, and the need and aching longing that had curled in his gut for weeks unwound with whipcord speed. He took her into his arms, found her mouth and ravaged it. The kiss went on and on and on until he realized he couldn't press her closer because he was still wearing his coat. And only one of her hands had come up to his shoulder...

Breaking away, he tried to defy his desire. "You're hurt. I don't want to make the pain worse."

"You won't make it worse. I just might need a little...help getting out of my clothes."

Her cheeks were rosy with an embarrassed flush that he found completely endearing. Unzipping his jacket, he tossed it over the banister, then lifted her in his arms and carried her up the stairs and into their bedroom.

Keeping in mind Faith's lack of experience, glad of it, he laid her on the bed gently. After he switched on the bedside lamp, he helped draw her sweater over her head. He'd seen her naked once...and that picture had burned itself permanently in his mind.

Her neck was beautifully curved, her shoulders straight and delicately feminine. So creamy pink. So kissable. He couldn't resist as he reached around her and unfastened her bra. She let it drop away, then she reached for the buttons on his flannel shirt.

"There are lots of things I can do with one hand," she said with a smile that made every nerve in his body come alive with anticipation.

It was torture, sitting on the side of the bed, waiting as she slipped each button through its hole. He felt the air on his chest; he longed for her touch. When she pulled his shirt from his waistband, they gazed at each other, engrossed in the moment.

Nick reached out and touched her breast...reverently, slowly, as if she might break. Feeling her breath hitch, he brought his eyes back to her face to make sure she was experiencing pleasure. He knew she was when she passed her hand over his chest, softly sifting through his hair, making him crazy with need.

"If this is how you can make me feel using one hand, we're going to be in real trouble when you can use two." Restraining his need, he tried to be casual. He wanted her to know she was pleasing him. He wanted to encourage her to be free with him, not restricted, not bound by any rules of propriety.

When Faith brushed her thumb slowly over his nipple, it became hard. "Let's get rid of the rest of our clothes," he murmured.

Faith slipped off her sneakers and he helped her with her jeans and panties. As she removed her socks, he stripped quickly and came down beside her.

"Nick, there are condoms in the nightstand," she almost whispered, taking him by surprise.

Practically speaking, birth control made sense. He knew the subject of more children would come up in their interviews with Darla. But they hadn't discussed it yet and he hadn't taken steps to prepare for it. Because he wanted that large family. Now wasn't the time to bring it up, not when they were so close to taking the final step to intimacy.

He reached inside the drawer and laid the packet at a convenient place.

Touching Faith was an erotic journey. Faith touching him was exquisite torment. When he kissed her lips and played with her tongue, she responded in kind. Each brush of his hand on her skin brought him more excitement, a harder arousal. Sliding her uninjured hand down his body, her fingers curled around him and he knew he could no longer prolong their pleasure.

Nick prepared himself then rose above her. "I don't want to hurt you."

Faith knew Nick was talking about her wrist...about the act itself. "You won't," she said as she stroked his jaw, oblivious to everything but him and the delicious way he made her feel.

When she'd decided downstairs that she wanted no more distance between them, no more tension, no more space in their bed, she'd known she was risking her heart. But she loved him, and she wouldn't withhold that love or her desire. Her body had ripened under his caresses and strokes, and now she knew she was ready for him and the future they could share. She brought his head down to her to tell him he didn't have to be so careful, to welcome him.

When he joined his body to hers, he took care, entering her slowly, and his tenderness cost him. She could tell from the tautness of his arms and the tension in his hips.

"Let go," she murmured into his ear. "I'm not made of glass."

Her words broke the dam. Nick thrust deep, his groan telling her his control was gone.

Nick's strong strokes lifted her from peak to peak of a glorious mountain. Digging her nails into his backside, she urged him on—harder, faster, higher. She cried his name when the pleasure became so great she couldn't contain her joy or her love. Seconds later, Nick found his release.

Both of them took gasping breaths until their breathing slowed. Then Nick leaned his forehead against hers. "That was worth waiting for."

After another slow, thorough kiss, he separated from her and lay beside her.

Faith curled up next to him, her head on his shoulder, her wrist throbbing again now that her adrenaline had diminished. She tentatively positioned her hand on his chest, knowing she should get ice, but not wanting to break the closeness.

With his thumb, he traced her fingers lightly. "How are you feeling?"

She didn't hesitate. "Wonderful."

He squeezed her firmly. "I mean your wrist. And don't tell me it's fine."

"It hurts," she said honestly.

Stroking her hair away from her face, he said, "I have to go get Jakie. Do you want ice first?"

She shook her head. "You get dressed. I'll get it. I don't want Jakie to worry."

Nick kissed her temple, then moved away and sat up. "I'm giving you fair warning. Not even ice on your wrist will keep me on my side of the bed tonight."

Bolder than she'd ever felt, she said with a coy smile, "I'm counting on it."

His look of surprise was replaced by an expression of pure male satisfaction, and Faith felt as if she were truly married.

Now all she had to do was hold onto the feeling...and Nick.

Chapter Ten

Rolls of Christmas wrap and spindles of red and green ribbon tumbled from the top shelf of her bedroom closet as Faith tried to pull a box from the shelf with one hand. But the spill of Christmas trimmings didn't faze her. She was too happy to care.

Last night after Nick had brought Jakie home, after they'd made sure he was sound asleep, they'd made love again and cuddled throughout the night. This morning he'd awakened her with a kiss and, a few minutes later, when the alarm had gone off, she'd hated leaving their bed.

After breakfast Nick had taken Jakie to school. She'd iced her wrist twice last night and again before breakfast. It would be difficult wrapping presents with one hand, but she had to get started. She'd managed to transfer most of the wrappings from the floor to the bed when she heard the front door open and close. As Nick's footsteps sounded on the stairs, her heart beat faster.

He stopped in the doorway, a smile on his face when he saw the paper and ribbons. "Need some help?"

"You don't have better things to do?" she teased.

The blaze of desire in his eyes, the one she'd recognized from last night, burned as brightly this morning. He came toward her slowly, each step a lovely anticipation of what might come. "I can think of one," he said, his voice going deeper. "Since we're alone in the house, we can make all the noise we want." Lifting her sweatshirt, he rested his hands on her waist, his thumbs making taunting circles on her midriff.

She forgot about ribbon and paper and gifts to be wrapped. If she could make one wish, it would be to live in this moment forever. To always feel as happy as she felt right now. "I won't have to whisper your name?" In the middle of the night, she had been aware of Jakie sleeping across the hall. They both had.

"Nope. In fact, you can shout it from the mountaintops." After he unfastened her bra, he caressed her breasts slowly, taunting her with anticipation.

"Nick," she said clearly, with all the desire she felt for him.

He took the hardening bud of her nipple between his thumb and forefinger. "Again," he commanded, watching her eyes, watching her face, watching passion begin to overtake her.

"Nick!" This time his name was even louder.

Bending his head, he kissed her, nibbling her lip, enticing her tongue into his mouth. Then he eased her back to the bed, lying down with her amid the bows and tags. He broke away to say, "Now let's see if we can't make that a shout."

Faith reached for him, knowing she might want too

much for Christmas this year. She prayed for Jakie to be her son. But she wanted something else, too.

Nick's love.

For now she'd take his passion and give hers, hoping in time love would follow.

Loaves of apple-cinnamon bread stood on racks on the counter, cooling and sending their aroma through the house. Nick had told her he liked all the smells that came from the kitchen.

Nick.

For the past six days she'd been so happy she felt as if she was floating on air. It had been like a honeymoon from the moment he'd carried her up the stairs. Nick would take Jakie to school in the mornings, then they'd make love. In the afternoons, she worked while Nick watched Jakie, or Nick worked or went into Burlington while she played with Jakie. And at night…they made love quietly but just as ardently as in the mornings. Over the weekend, they'd found time to do last-minute Christmas shopping along with overseeing practices for the pageant.

Dress rehearsal was tomorrow night, December 23. She intended to give the loaves of bread she'd baked as presents to all the people who had helped with the pageant. The following night was Christmas Eve and the performance.

When the phone rang, she switched off the oven. Maybe it was Nick.

Don't be silly, she told herself. He'd gone into Burlington again to look at more locations.

After they'd made love.

She was smiling when she picked up the phone and said hello.

"Faith, it's Darla Granger. I have news you're going to like very much."

"What?"

"The Brewers are pregnant! Can you believe it? After all these years."

Faith's heart pounded. "What does that mean for us?"

"It means that you and Nick have clear sailing. They only care about the child Mrs. Brewer is carrying. I think they realized all along Jakie is attached to you, but they wanted a child so badly they focused on him and wouldn't let go. Now they have. Merry Christmas, Faith. I'll be in touch with you again after the holidays."

Faith hung up the phone and stared at it a few moments, then whooped with joy. Jakie was going to be their son. He really was!

Wait until Nick heard. He'd be so happy.

Wouldn't he?

A fleeting thought flashed in her mind. He'd married her for Jakie's sake. Maybe now that the threat of his being taken away had passed...

She pushed the doubts away. They were building a life. They were building a family.

But insecurities niggled at her.

Christmas would be wonderful this year, she reminded herself.

And she suddenly made a decision. She would hold onto the news until Christmas. It would be a wonderful gift to give Nick—the joy of knowing Jakie would be theirs.

She would tell him on Christmas morning.

The staple gun snapped into the wooden door frame as Nick attached the last of the Christmas lights. A little late to be putting up the outside decorations. Next year, he'd try to decorate earlier. He expected Faith to come home with Jakie at any moment, and he'd wanted to have the outside of the house finished before lunch. They were going to the community center this afternoon to make sure everything was ready for dress rehearsal tonight.

Looking to the gray sky, he felt snow in the air. The weatherman was predicting snow on Christmas Eve. It would be the perfect topping for a special night.

Every night was special these days with last-minute shopping trips, baking cookies, sitting around the fire playing with Jakie...making love. It was everything Nick had ever dreamed of.

He opened the door and went inside, appreciating the Christmas decorations Faith had put around, the three stockings hanging from the mantel, the lingering scent of the bacon from breakfast, the warmth that always enveloped him like a down quilt on a winter night. After he took off his jacket, he went upstairs to check the answering machine. Anything could happen at the store this time of year, and he wanted to make sure he was available.

The light blinked, and he pressed the button.

"Faith, this is Darla. I just wanted to tell you all your paperwork is in order. Everything is here and complete. I bet you couldn't wait to tell Nick about the Brewers' pregnancy. As I told you yesterday, I'll get back to you after the holidays."

It took a moment for Darla's message to register. Nick played it back, wanting to make sure he'd heard it correctly.

He had.

Darla had talked with Faith yesterday, and Faith hadn't told him. And the Brewers were pregnant? Did that mean they'd lost interest in Jakie?

Why hadn't Faith told him?

Suddenly he felt cold, as if a bitter wind had swept into the house. He remembered Pam and her deception. Her lie. Faith's omission was a lie. It was a betrayal. She hadn't told him because she didn't want him to know.

Why?

All he could think about was Pam, lying to him, telling him she was pregnant when she wanted to get him to marry her. Women and lies—did they go together? He'd believed Faith was different...

He and Faith had married because of the threat of Jakie being taken away from her. Did she believe if that threat was gone he'd leave? Is that why she hadn't told him? What other explanation could there be?

She didn't trust him.

He remembered her hesitancy to make their marriage real in the complete sense of the word. He remembered her suspicions about Kathleen. And now she was keeping something this important from him.

The front door opened and he heard her voice, then Jakie's. He had to talk to her and he had to talk to her *now*. Going downstairs, he forced himself to keep the anger at bay.

"Jakie, can you watch a video for a few minutes. I have to talk to Faith upstairs."

Faith closed the closet door. "I was going to make lunch—"

"I need to speak with you. This can't wait."

With a puzzled look, she studied him. "All right.

Jakie, why don't you watch the one we taped last night? I'll set it up for you."

Nick returned to Faith's office and paced.

A few minutes later, she reached the hall and saw him. "The front of the house looks nice. Maybe we can—"

He pointed to the answering machine. "You have a message. Play it."

The tone of his voice must have told her not to argue with him. Stepping into the room, she pressed the Play button and listened. As Darla's message played, she grew pale.

"Why didn't you tell me?" he asked, the anger coming closer to the surface, battling for release.

"I was going to," she said softly.

"When?" he snapped. "Next week? Next month?"

"On Christmas morning. I thought it would be a wonderful gift. The Brewers aren't interested in adopting anymore and..."

"I figured that out. But I've figured you out, too. You don't know how to trust. And because you don't, you weren't honest with me. Honesty in a marriage is everything, Faith. I should know. My first one didn't last because my wife lied to me. Once trust is broken, it can't be fixed."

"But I *do* trust you. I..."

"If you trusted me, you wouldn't keep anything hidden from me. For any length of time. Face reality, Faith. You didn't tell me because you were afraid I'd leave. You were afraid my promise didn't mean anything now that you could probably adopt Jakie on your own if you wanted to." He could tell by the expression on her face that he was right.

But she took him off guard when she said, "Trust

goes two ways, Nick. You told me you divorced Pamela Ann. But you never said why. Does that mean you didn't trust me?''

"No. It means I didn't want you to know what a fool I was...or how easily she manipulated me. She wanted to get serious. I didn't. I wanted out of Winding Creek, and she knew it. Instead of accepting it, she took advantage of the one time we made love without birth control and a month later told me she was pregnant. Only she wasn't."

"You married her because you thought she was pregnant," Faith murmured, as if she finally understood.

"Oh, yes. And she was hoping she *would* get pregnant before I found out she'd lied. Only she didn't get pregnant, I saw no changes in her body and I guessed the truth. End of marriage. End of story."

"She trapped you."

"Exactly. And in a way, you were trying to do the same thing."

Faith looked horrified. "No! I'd never do that. I just wanted a couple of days in case..."

"In case I left."

Clasping his arm, trying to use her touch—the touch he'd so wanted—to make him understand, she said, "Nick, you didn't marry me because you couldn't live without me. You married me because of a crisis with Jakie. The crisis is over. You were married to Pamela Ann for a few months. You told me *you* divorced *her*. Then you didn't tell anyone about our marriage. Yes, I was afraid you'd leave."

The anger he'd been carrying all these years, the sense of betrayal, Faith's doubts, all exploded as he tore away from her. "I told you I keep my promises.

But you can't believe in me because you don't believe in yourself."

The phone rang and they just stared at it, both of them frozen. When the machine clicked on, Nick heard his manager's voice.

"Nick, it's Greg. We have trouble. I caught a cashier taking money from the register. Do you want me to call the cops? Get back to me as soon as—"

Nick snatched up the phone. "I'm here. Tell me what happened."

Faith's marriage was crumbling before her. She could see it in Nick's eyes, feel the anger emanating from every rigid movement of his body, see it in his set jaw. Her hands trembled and she stuffed them into her jeans' pockets, still feeling a twinge in her wrist, remembering making love for the first time and every time after. She loved him so. Her thoughts ran rampant, and it wasn't until Nick hung up the phone that she realized she hadn't even listened to the conversation.

"I have to leave for Rutland." The expression on his face was even colder than before.

"Now?"

"Sooner than now. Greg doesn't know how long an employee has been taking money or exactly how much. We have to go through records and decide how we're going to deal with this. You and I can't settle anything now. We both need some time. This will give it to us." He headed for the bedroom.

She followed him. "Jakie's counting on you to be here for the pageant."

Not facing her, he kept moving. "I don't know what's going to happen, Faith. Especially if we file charges. I don't want to disappoint Jakie, but I have to handle this myself."

When Nick took his suitcase from the closet, she wished she could say something that would keep him here. If she could only do something. Clasping his arm again, she said, "Nick, I'm sorry. I never meant to hurt you. I never meant to keep anything from you."

Nick's arm went stiff before he pulled away, rejecting her explanation. "But you did." Tossing the travel bag onto the bed, he unzipped it. "I'll talk to Jakie and try to explain why I'm leaving."

"Would you be leaving if you hadn't received that phone call?" She couldn't help holding her breath while she waited for his answer.

His voice was gruff. "I don't know."

It was obvious that he'd closed her out. Nothing she said now would make a difference. Not even if she told him she loved him. Because he wouldn't believe her. Apparently trust was more important to Nick than love, and she'd broken that trust.

This morning their bedroom had been the best place in the world to be. Now, it hurt so badly to stand there and watch Nick pack, that she had to walk away. Standing in the doorway for a moment, she waited to see if he'd look at her, if he'd tell her they could work everything out.

But he kept packing.

She went downstairs to Jakie, determined to hold back her tears.

The chaos at The Toy Station the day before Christmas could only be rivaled by the turmoil inside Nick as he stood at his office window, gazing at the falling snow. He couldn't stop thinking about Faith...and Jakie. His anger had subsided, leaving him with a sense of devastating loss that was even worse. Thank God he'd had a crisis to focus on.

But even through the interview with his employee who'd been voiding sales and pocketing the cash for the past two months, he couldn't forget the expression on Faith's face when he'd walked out the door.

Damn, he didn't know what to do.

The apartment upstairs that he used to call home had been even more silent and empty than the last time he'd returned—before his wedding. There were no smells of home cooking, no patter of Jakie's feet, no one beside him in his bed. But marriage had to be so much more than all that. It had to be respect and partnership and honesty and...

After a sharp rap, his office door opened and his manager walked in. "I got Virginia set up on a repayment plan for what she took and the money you loaned her. She was still crying when she left. She told me to tell you again how thankful she is that you didn't call the police and that you're willing to give her more hours."

Turning from the window, Nick pulled out the leather chair at his desk and sank into it as he examined the man who practically knew as much about The Toy Station and its workings as he did. Greg was tall and lanky with wire-rimmed glasses that constantly slipped down his nose. He knew his manager was married, but he didn't know much else about his personal life.

Nick leaned back against the black leather. "Calling the police wouldn't have helped anyone. It wouldn't have paid her son's medical bills or helped her make ends meet. Virginia doesn't need a police record. She needs support checks from a deadbeat husband. I can't imagine how she's fed and clothed her two kids as long as she has. I just wish she'd come to me sooner and asked for help."

"Desperation drives people to do uncharacteristic things," Greg said as he sat on the chair in front of Nick's desk. "She didn't know you, Nick. She didn't know you'd try to help if you could."

"I remember what it's like not to have any family around, no one to give you a boost when you think you're too tired to keep trying."

"You gave her a boost. And I think Virginia's the type of woman who will make the most of it. She won't let you down."

The confidence in Greg's voice made Nick realize how detached he'd become from everyone before he returned to Winding Creek. Why didn't he know Greg better? Why didn't he know the people who worked for him? "You know our employees. I don't."

Greg shrugged. "I'm on the floor more than you are." Glancing at his watch, he said, "It's almost closing time. You've got a long drive. If you want me to batten down the hatches..."

"I'm not sure if I'm going back tonight."

The surprise on Greg's face was obvious. "It's Christmas Eve."

An ache inside Nick hurt so bad he grimaced. "Yeah, I know. Tell me something. How long have you been married?"

"Almost four years."

"Have you ever thought of walking away?"

"Sure, I have."

"Why don't you?"

His manager could tell the question wasn't an idle one. "My parents will be celebrating their fortieth wedding anniversary soon. My dad always said to me a real man doesn't love just when it's convenient. He loves for a lifetime. I guess it stuck. If two people love each other, I think they can solve anything.''

Love.

It wasn't a concept Nick knew very much about. Matter of fact, he'd wiped it from his vocabulary. His mother had shown her love by leaving. His father had forgotten love in favor of a bottle. And Pam's love...

"Nick, I know I might be overstepping my bounds, but if you and your wife had a fight, you're not going to solve anything by being here. Distance only creates more distance." When Nick didn't respond, Greg said, "I'd better get back to the service desk. Let me know if you want me to close."

His office door shut with a *click*.

Distance only creates more distance.

A real man doesn't love just when it's convenient.

Jakie's counting on you to be here for the pageant.

Nick couldn't forget Jakie's eyes when he'd told him he had to leave. He couldn't forget Faith opening her life to him, making him part of it. Defending him to her mother. Trembling when he touched her. Making love to him as if...

As if she loved him.

No longer could he deny his feeling of wanting to be around her night and day, of needing her smiles as much as her body, of dreaming of more children with her.

It was love. He loved her, too.

He'd thought they only needed respect for each other and trust. But he'd forgotten about love.

In retrospect, he realized she'd given her heart along with her body despite her doubts, despite her fears. He remembered the condoms she'd bought because she *didn't* want to trap him. And loving him, she'd wanted a couple more days of happiness just in case...

Just in case he didn't love her. She couldn't give him her trust because she didn't know what he felt.

What had Faith said? That trust goes both ways. If he'd trusted her, he would have told her about Pam. Was she right? His marriage to Faith had happened so fast. She thought he'd married her simply to protect Jakie. No doubt that was the catalyst. But even if there had been no Jakie, after seeing Faith again, experiencing her kindness, acknowledging the desire... He might have found another excuse to stay in Winding Creek. He definitely would have returned.

Yes, he loved her. When, where, why it had happened, that he wasn't sure of. But it *had* happened, and she didn't know it. She thought he wanted a family. She thought he wanted to satisfy his physical needs. She thought he had never learned how to make a commitment. All of it seemed so clear now. He hadn't told her how much she meant to him because he'd been protecting himself against the possibility that their marriage wouldn't succeed.

He hadn't told Greg about his marriage because he wasn't sure about it himself. He hadn't been sure he could be the husband Faith needed or the father Jakie needed. It wasn't only Faith's insecurities that had put a barrier between them. It was his own. Not deciding on the location for the second store was just a symptom of his own lack of confidence to make a commitment that would last a lifetime.

And now he'd done the one thing Faith had been afraid of most. He'd walked out when he should have stayed.

Could she ever forgive him for that? For putting distance between them so he didn't have to deal with his anger, their argument, the feeling that she'd betrayed him? All his life he'd relied on distance to cope with pain. It didn't work because the pain didn't go away and the distance created a loneliness that was impossible to conquer.

He had to get to the pageant. He had to keep his promise to Jakie that he'd be there. He had to ask Faith to forgive him. Before it was too late.

Snow blindness. Again. On another crucial day in his life.

Nick cursed the storm that couldn't give Vermont a frosting, but rather had to dump another foot of snow for Christmas. If he hadn't stopped at the jewelry store...

The roads would still be treacherous. He'd still be trying to follow a set of taillights to stay on the asphalt.

All of a sudden, the lights in front of Nick swerved. Even through the hum of the heater and the snow muffling outside noises, he heard the crunch of metal as the car in front of him plowed into another car stranded alongside the road.

If he stopped, he wouldn't get to the pageant. Faith would think his promise meant nothing. It would be harder for her to forgive him...

He had to stop. Someone in the car could be hurt. He really had no choice.

But would Faith understand?

The orange flames of the firelight leapt into the darkness of the chimney as Faith sat on the floor in front of them trying to get warm. The heat of the fire fought against the cold deep inside her as she rubbed her hands over the long sleeves of her red velvet jumpsuit. She'd bought it specifically for tonight...for Nick....

Hoping against hope, she'd watched for him throughout the pageant as she'd fielded questions from her mother, directed the children and admired Bud and Margie's new baby girl. They'd named her Noel.

Faith blamed her burning eyes on the heat from the fire. But when a tear trickled down her cheek, she knew she couldn't hold them back any longer. Jakie had gotten caught up in the pageant, in being the best angel he knew how to be. But after she'd read him the Christmas story, after she'd pulled his covers up to his chin, he'd asked if Nick would be home in the morning. She'd had to tell him she didn't know.

If only Nick had told her about his first marriage. If only she hadn't been so afraid of losing him. If only...

At first she thought she heard the old house creaking. But then there was definite noise on the porch, a key in the lock. The next moment the door opened and Nick stood in the foyer. Only the lights on the tree illuminated the darkness. She couldn't see his face, and she didn't know whether to go to him or to wait for him to come to her. Before she could swipe the tears from her cheeks, he'd made the decision for her by coming into the room, shrugging out of his jacket and sitting on the hearth across from her.

He looked uncomfortable as he rested his hands on his jean-clad thighs and studied her in the firelight. "How'd the pageant go?"

Finding her voice was almost as difficult as attempting to slow her pulse. "It went well with some prompting here and there."

"Was Jakie terribly disappointed I didn't show up?"

"He just doesn't understand..." she trailed off, afraid Nick had only returned because of Jakie.

"No, I guess not. Neither did I."

Guilt stabbed her. She wanted to reach out to her husband but was afraid he wouldn't want her to. "Nick, I'm sorry. I know that doesn't mean much to you, but I don't know what else to say or how to regain your trust."

A log popped in the silence. Then in a deep, husky voice, he said, "You don't have to regain my trust. I was a jerk. I overreacted. And if I'd realized sooner how much I love you, and if I'd told you, none of this would have happened."

His words took her breath away. "You love me?"

Taking her hand, he tugged her up on her knees. "How could I not love you? Oh, Faith, I hadn't felt anything for so long I didn't know what love was. That's not a very good excuse, and I don't know if you can ever forgive me for walking out like that. But I promise I will never do it again. Will you give me another chance? Give us another chance?"

His question chased the cold away. She felt warm again, filled with hope. "I prayed you'd come back. I prayed you'd forgive me. I love you so much, Nick. I just wanted to hold on to the happiness we'd found."

He took her face in his hands. "We'll hold onto it together."

When his lips met hers, he held nothing back. There was passion and promise and no barriers to either. Faith wrapped her arms around Nick, giving and taking, forgiving, and asking for the same forgiveness. They pledged their love without words, renewing their vows, accepting each other's flaws as well as their gifts.

Nick raised his head and wiped his thumb over her

tearstained cheek. "I tried to get back in time for the pageant. But there was an accident and I stopped. By the time the police and an ambulance got there, I was already too late."

Faith knew Nick was the type of man who had to stop and help. That was one reason she loved him so, along with a trillion others. "Was anyone injured badly?"

"Mostly cuts and bruises. I just wanted you to know I didn't deliberately miss the pageant." Reaching into his shirt pocket, he took out a small box. "I want to give you your Christmas present now."

"You've given me my Christmas present," she murmured, still trying to absorb the wonder of his love.

He smiled and opened the velvet box. "Something a little more tangible."

The emerald-cut diamond reflected the firelight as she stared at it in stunned surprise. "It's beautiful!"

After he took it from the box, he clasped her hand and slid the ring onto her finger above the plain gold band. "Merry Christmas, Faith. When you look at this ring, know how much I love you."

Feeling a freedom she'd never felt before, she stroked his jaw, looked into his eyes, then kissed him with all the love in her heart. He accepted her kiss and her love, finally standing with her and leading her to the sofa. Enfolding her in his arms, he kissed her again deeply, promising her many more Christmases and a lifetime of love.

Epilogue

Seventeen months later

Pink, blue and yellow balloons bobbed in the May breeze inside the enclosed porch. Nick tossed a ball to Jakie in their backyard. The seven-year-old hit it and it grounded out to Tom. Faith's father had insisted on joining in the pitch-catch session even though his arthritis was acting up. Bud, his sons and Greg Blumfield stood farther back in the yard, ready to catch deeper hits.

"Good hit, Jakie," Nick called.

"Thanks, Dad."

The title made Nick feel proud. As he thought about why they were giving this party today, why Faith was bringing a sheet cake through the back door, followed by Darla Granger with ice cream, Constance with a pot of coffee, Greg's wife carrying presents and Margie holding Noel, his chest tightened with emotion. Today, it was official. Today, he and Faith had legally become Jakie's parents.

"C'mon, everyone," Faith called, her smile as bright as Nick had ever seen it. "Now that you've worked off the hamburgers and hot dogs, we have dessert."

In the past year and a half, he and Faith had learned more about parenting and the outside assistance that adoptive parents and children needed throughout the process. They'd attended a support group, and Constance and Tom had even gone along now and then. They'd developed even stronger friendships with Margie and Bud and new bonds with Greg and his wife. Nick now knew a whole lot more about connection rather than detachment. And he liked it.

He and Faith had also grown into a deeper sense of love for each other. He'd never forget their first Christmas Eve when they'd truly sealed their vows…or their first Christmas morning together as a family. After making love on the sofa, he and Faith had fallen asleep only to be awakened by Jakie at five in the morning. He'd come downstairs to find out if Santa had arrived. But he'd seemed less thrilled by the presents under the tree than the fact Faith and Nick were sleeping on the sofa under the colorful quilt.

"You're home!" he'd shouted coming to Nick for a big hug.

"I sure am," Nick had said, feeling it deep in his soul. "Why don't you go back upstairs and brush your teeth. Then we can make breakfast and open presents."

"All right!" Jakie had agreed and scurried upstairs.

Faith had blushed from her head to her toes, thanked

him for being a quick thinker and scrambled into her clothes. He'd given her a kiss they couldn't consummate until that night, but no Christmas had ever been so special or so happy. Looking at his wife now, Nick was filled with the same desire that had persisted since the day he'd returned to Winding Creek.

As everyone followed Faith's directive to gather on the porch, Constance stepped into the backyard and took Nick aside. "I saw that bicycle you bought for Jakie as an adoption present."

"And?" He'd realized that Constance would never hesitate to speak her mind, but he'd come to respect her and love her with the same devotion he would have given his own mother.

"And I think it's just right for riding around your neighborhood. Though, I do think you've got to plant more trees. These new developments are so barren."

Nick chuckled. When he and Faith had decided to buy a bigger house on the outskirts of Winding Creek, Constance had told them everything she liked about the house and everything she thought could use improvement. "What kind do you suggest?"

"Silver maples. They grow the fastest. As if you need my suggestion," she added with a smile. "You know, Nick, I was wrong about you. You're good for my daughter. She's happy, more confident."

"She's good for me."

Faith came through the door. "Is this a private conversation or are you deciding which flavor ice cream you'd like with your cake?"

"No deciding there," Constance said casually. "Chocolate all the way. I'll go start scooping."

"Anything I should know about?" Faith asked Nick with a concerned look as her mother went inside.

"Nope. Your mom just told me I'm good for you. I think my charm is finally winning her over."

"Your love for me and Jakie is," Faith suggested in a gentle way.

Nick couldn't refrain from curving his arm around his wife and kissing her. When he straightened, he saw the look of love in her eyes that he treasured so carefully. Their life was full of each other, Jakie, family and friends. Even his dad called more, had shown up for Easter with them. Life couldn't get much better.

"When I went to the drugstore this morning, I bought something besides balloons," Faith said.

"Am I supposed to guess?" he teased.

"I think I'm pregnant, Nick. I got a pregnancy test."

"Did you use it?" He felt the love inside him blooming into a feeling he could hardly contain.

"I didn't want to take away from Jakie's party. I thought we could do it tonight if you want to be there."

"If I want to *be* there? You bet I want to be there, Mrs. Clark. Tonight…and when we're changing diapers…when we get up for night feedings…when Jakie graduates from grade school, high school and college. I want to be there always."

"Always. What a wonderful word."

He kissed her again to thank her for inviting him into her life, to thank her for loving him, to thank her for helping him become Jakie's father.

Late that night after Jakie was tucked into bed and sound asleep, Faith showed the stick to Nick. There were two bright pink lines!

She threw her arms around him. "Congratulations, Dad."

Swinging her into his arms, he carried her to their bed and turned off the light.

Dreams did come true.

*   *   *   *   *

Take 4 bestselling love stories FREE

Plus get a FREE surprise gift!

Special Limited-time Offer

Mail to Silhouette Reader Service™

3010 Walden Avenue
P.O. Box 1867
Buffalo, N.Y. 14240-1867

YES! Please send me 4 free Silhouette Romance™ novels and my free surprise gift. Then send me 6 brand-new novels every month, which I will receive months before they appear in bookstores. Bill me at the low price of $2.67 each plus 25¢ delivery and applicable sales tax, if any.* That's the complete price and a savings of over 10% off the cover prices—quite a bargain! I understand that accepting the books and gift places me under no obligation ever to buy any books. I can always return a shipment and cancel at any time. Even if I never buy another book from Silhouette, the 4 free books and the surprise gift are mine to keep forever.

215 BPA A3UT

Name	(PLEASE PRINT)
Address	Apt. No.
City	State	Zip

This offer is limited to one order per household and not valid to present Silhouette Romance™ subscribers. *Terms and prices are subject to change without notice. Sales tax applicable in N.Y.

USROM-696   ©1990 Harlequin Enterprises Limited

CHRISTINE FLYNN

Continues the twelve-book
series—36 HOURS—in
December 1997 with
Book Six

FATHER AND CHILD REUNION

Eve Stuart was back, and Rio Redtree couldn't ignore the fact
that her daughter bore his Native American features. So, Eve
had broken his heart *and* kept him from his child! But this
was no time for grudges, because his little girl and her
mother, the woman he had never stopped—could never stop—
loving, were in danger, and Rio would stop at nothing to
protect *his* family.

For Rio and Eve and *all* the residents of Grand Springs,
Colorado, the storm-induced blackout was just the beginning
of 36 Hours that changed *everything!* You won't want to
miss a single book.

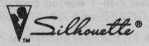

Available at your favorite retail outlet.

Welcome to the Towers!

In January
New York Times bestselling author

takes us to the fabulous Maine coast mansion
haunted by a generations-old secret and introduces
us to the fascinating family that lives there.

Mechanic Catherine "C.C." Calhoun and hotel magnate
Trenton St. James mix like axle grease and mineral
water—until they kiss. Efficient Amanda Calhoun finds
easygoing Sloan O'Riley insufferable—and irresistible.
And they all must race to solve the mystery
surrounding a priceless hidden emerald necklace.

Catherine and Amanda

THE Calhoun Women

**A special 2-in-1 edition containing
COURTING CATHERINE and A MAN FOR AMANDA.**

Look for the next installment of
THE CALHOUN WOMEN with Lilah and Suzanna's
stories, coming in March 1998.

Available at your favorite retail outlet.

Return to the Towers!

In March
New York Times bestselling author

NORA ROBERTS

brings us to the Calhouns' fabulous
Maine coast mansion and reveals the
tragic secrets hidden there for generations.

For all his degrees, Professor Max Quartermain has a
lot to learn about love—and luscious Lilah Calhoun is
just the woman to teach him. Ex-cop Holt Bradford is
as prickly as a thornbush—until Suzanna Calhoun's
special touch makes love blossom in his heart.
And all of them are caught in the race to solve
the generations-old mystery of a priceless
lost necklace...and a timeless love.

Lilah and Suzanna
THE
Calhoun Women

A special 2-in-1 edition containing
FOR THE LOVE OF LILAH and
SUZANNA'S SURRENDER

Available at your favorite retail outlet.